BACKWARD
GLANCE

Wordrunner Press
Petaluma, California
www.wordrunner.com/publish

BACKWARD GLANCE

A Storyteller's Compendium

TALES

OF

FARAWAY AND EVERYDAY
LOVE AND WAR
CHANCE AND DESTINY
WHAT WE CALL LIFE

LUM FRANCO

Acknowledgements

To writer, mentor and patient gardener, Guy Biederman, whose writing seeds nurtured characters and situations into stories of varying voice, pace and place, I give many, many thanks. Without your guidance I wouldn't have discovered so much within and without.

To the tellers of tales I was privileged to hear and to learn from by listening, my gratitude for sharing what was yours. From your words sprang other stories different in depiction and detail, cast and circumstance.

To the proofreader, prod, prompt, and wit whose unfailing support, perception and storytelling verve widened my world, my thanks for all the things you do and give without measure.

This potpourri of short fiction is dedicated to those named and unnamed with the intent of doing right by you.

Looking Back

My mother's bed was of brown metal. The foot was arched, rods of varying length propped up the curve. The head frame was a higher arch with taller struts, but I mostly saw the foot. Dusty spring coils squeaked if I jumped too hard on the mattress.

An open metal canister with a curled lip and two thick hooks to latch onto the bed frame provided light. The switch was a big knob that turned. The flat seamed cord, an army brown like the lamp case, ran in a diagonal behind the bed.

When I was allowed to stay up late, I'd lie on my mother's side of the double bed with the light on and a Golden Book, one of many my big brother gave me. One of my big sisters would come to shut off the light and tell me to go to sleep, then I would move to my side of the bed against the wall, painted a green unlike any other green I saw anywhere else.

I was born in that bed. I slept there until I got to be too big to be there anymore. I learned to look beyond the foot arch, past the bureau mirror and out the door to the hallway. I learned to look back.

CONTENTS

CONTENTS *(continued)*

CONTENTS *(continued)*

What We Call Life

Faraway
and
Everyday

Summer Afternoon

The sky still glowered as the noon bells rang. When the last dish was washed and dried, a sliver of light sneaked beneath wan clouds. Later, sun smoked off black asphalt, shimmered in leafy droplets, glazed blank windows. From the kitchen alcove, Marco watched green hills tinged with the fragility of spring absorb the gold of summer.

"Let's go for a ride," he said to his father.

Vigi sat on the veranda lined with red geraniums. A stub of a cigarette trembled between fingers thick as cigars. He wore a faded blue shirt, once good enough to go into town and still too good to tend the vines. His clear blue eyes questioned his firstborn, a visitor come from afar.

"Out to La Tesa. The colors, they're beautiful."

Vigi jabbed at gray ash and white butts until burning red died black. "Time was, a rainbow crossed the sky behind each summer storm. Bright, clear bands. Colors sharp, so sharp they hurt the eyes." Vigi grasped the arms of the metal chair, heaved himself up. When he knew his legs would hold him, his hands let go. "I'll change my shirt."

Sun-brown fingers gripped the roof of the Fiat as Vigi lifted a stiff leg. The other hand held the rim of the door to steady shifting weight. His elbow resonated to the beat of his heart, faster than the beat he'd drummed for dancing GIs when they were all young, the world fresh from war.

Marco followed the state road past the white palace where they'd once worked as sharecroppers. They drove up a rise past the red brick castle. Asphalt ran into gravel,

1

petered out. Vigi waved to tractor tracks gutting muddy soil. "That way." They lurched to a stop at a clearing open to sky and sound. Below, the valley unfolded, unhurried green all the way to the milky sea.

"Let's take a look at the vineyards. Schiopetto's wine is famous now," Marco said.

Vigi shoved the door open, lifted his hand to grip the window, then let it drop to his lap. A breeze swept the fresh scent of rain-wet earth into the car, tugged at Vigi's sleeve. "I'll wait here, smoke a cigarette." He glanced from his son to the clearing edged with stems and stalks sheathed in sunlight. "Go ahead, look again on La Tesa."

Marco's eyes ranged the hill. Tucked between knobby knuckles, a small swatch of vines soaked up sun, snug from wind and frost. La Tesa. That fertile but distant plot had been granted to Vigi by the estate administrator. What the land rendered was his to keep, and it rendered well under his able hands.

A whiff from the sea laced the air with the scent of far-away places. Marco stretched his gaze, remembered crisp mornings watching his father's shoulders rise and fall as they walked to La Tesa. Damp soil squeezed between his toes, one hand held the tether, the other rested on the cow's warm flank. Viola snorted as she worked her head side to side, the empty cart creaking as the sky cracked open to new sun.

Marco blinked at the brightness. Leaves rustled, grass nodded. He turned, startled. Vigi stood, unsteady, at the edge. Around him light swirled, wind tussled.

Once again shoulder to shoulder, father and son reveled in a green world suffused with a gold gentle as love.

Faint at first, bells sounded in fitful gusts, their ringing called to others until the bells of their village answered.

Vigi turned, his clear blue eyes luminous with wonder. "Never, in all my life, have I seen a day with such light as today."

MAY ROSES

Back when cherry trees, all different kinds—cream, orange, crimson—crisscrossed fields to the furthest farmhouse, back when Il Duce's electricity reached the village but before the Blackshirts did, a young woman by the name of Gisela lived up among the chestnuts and acacias on the hill behind the castle. Gone now, that old place. Even the hill's changed, bulldozed smooth and faceless to make grape growing easier.

Benessere has come to Friuli. The good life also brought along cement posts stiff as whiskers bristling in vineyards instead of posts of acacia. Best wood to hold vines. Took time, attention, sitting by the fogolar in winter cold, working by firelight, stripping and chipping acacia branches. Nowadays, time matters, details don't.

Gisela's not a common name, then or now, but wasn't out of place. Family were sharecroppers like most. Gisela was as lucky just as her sister Teresa was not. Hair wet from washing, Teresa stood at a high open window. Dark clouds stormed up the valley. Her mother in the garden below, her father in the barn. The sky crackled, air sizzled. Thunder clapped, left a stench. Teresa's burnt body slumped over the window frame. A disgrazia, villagers said. A misfortune.

Maybe that lightning bolt gave Gisela a chance. Landed a job at the cotton mill. Hard work, but steady. Down the hill she trudged in her zoccoli, then wedged the wooden clogs in a tree by the muddy path. She put on her shoes and rode her bicycle to the factory in Pudigora, some kilometers away.

Fine bones, nice white teeth, small and straight. A sweet smile, and a frequent one. No wonder Fino took to her. The older brother of Claudio Beciar, the butcher, Fino set his eyes on Gisela early on. Courted her long and steady. About the only steady thing Fino did. A talker more than a worker, Fino tilled the soil without breaking much sweat. A sharecropper without much luck, he said. Others thought a farmer without much will.

To hear him tell it at the tavern, Fino was the best and first at just about everything. Lord to his companions at the osteria, he bought them drinks with promises to pay. A man who thought himself worthy of better but the chance to prove it never came. At harvest, nothing much was left after surrendering half to the landowner and squaring accounts with barkeep and seed seller. For Gisela, another promise for a wedding next harvest.

Gisela, dazzled by Fino's fine talk and broad shoulders, held true to him and the memory of their youth together. Human nature being what it is, Gisela gave birth in midwinter. A girl. After the allotted time, Gisela went back to work at the cotton mill. Her mother cared for the baby.

Fino courted Gisela as before. On Sundays after dinner he walked from the village where he lived with Claudio above the meat shop to the hill where Gisela's house stood among fields and vineyards. Easy to see the flow of the seasons from the courtyard, the hill flank planted with row after row of vines, barren brown or bursting into leaf or burdened with grapes.

Being a factory worker is easier than being a farmwife. Gisela, a mother now, saw what she earned and what she could give her daughter. Saw Fino with different eyes.

What he could provide, what he could do. Childhood sweethearts, they were. So she bided her time.

A middleman, that's what he would be, Fino's grand scheme to earn enough for a grand wedding feast. Farmers he knew with calves and piglets to sell and him the brother of the butcher, surely he could broker the exchanges for a fee.

As fate would have it, the supervisor of the cotton mill liked Gisela's smile, her rich laugh and her steadfast ways. A man with a good heart, he offered her a future, a home for her and her baby, if given the chance.

Gisela thought more and more about Fino. It was Sunday, the hour of courtship. There was a knock at the door. Gisela threw a black shawl over her shoulders, the long fringe a fan against her pale arms. She and Fino walked among the vines, rich in leaf. At the head of each row, a bush thick with thorns and fat buds promised roses of pink, red, white. Twilight heady with the scent of promise.

Gisela questioned her sweetheart of youth. A wedding at summer's end she wanted. Again, Fino shrugged his broad shoulders. Unlucky he was. Seeded late, missed the first rain, seedlings didn't take. The oldtimers predicted a good season, but his crops would not feed two.

Worse, his scheme to act as middleman came to naught. Another, one from Moraro, had moved more quickly, brokered deals between farmer and butcher. Their wedded life together was sure to begin after the next harvest.

Gisela stood rooted to the soil, the sound of night wings whirring in the air. She looked at Fino, his even features, thick curls caressing broad forehead, and saw the boy who stole her heart when she was but a girl. For a moment that Delfino of memory entranced her. A flicker of light in the night sky, the muffled sound of a distant storm rolled up the valley to their hills, cleared the air. Gisela made up her mind. She would wait no longer. She would marry another.

Fino refused to believe. Pride armed him with words, promises. Gisela stood firm. They parted. The following Sunday at the hour of courtship Fino left his room above the butcher shop and walked to the osteria. Another Sunday passed. Still, Fino could not swallow it.

On a Saturday evening as the hills closed over the sun with ribbons of cyclamen and rose, Fino walked a familiar path. Gisela came to the door, saw him standing in the dusk, his arm laden with roses, red, wild, full-petaled, tangled in thorns and leaves. And the scent, the swelling scent, sweetened the air, softened Gisela's stance. She agreed to walk with him once more. She would not be long she told her mother.

Later, when the perfume of the earth slipped into the thickness of night, Claudio Beciar heard Fino go to his room. Claudio closed his eyes inviting sleep to return. An explosion filled him with fear. Fino lay in his bed, face to the wall. Even for the butcher the blood splattered against wall, staining plank floor, was too much.

Then fear came again to Claudio, he took the path Fino had taken. Carabinieri and friends followed, lanterns aloft. Gisela's parents awakened, frightened not to find Gisela next to her sleeping child. Calling Gisela's name, searchers fanned from farmyard to fields.

Sunday, the bells rang as they always ring for Mass. Villagers knotted in twos and threes outside the church. The voice ran fast and quick of Fino and his end. Then a single searcher rushed into the church. The middle bell began to toll, its sweet voice light as a woman's laugh lifted into the morning, reached a distant farmhouse, white amid green.

There, just as dawn touched the tips of the hills, searchers had walked through a vineyard thick with leaf. Freshening day picked at a white fleck against darkness. Gisela lay on the ground, arm outflung, fingers caressing black soil, mouth open. Her fine white teeth kissed the earth. Red roses, fresh with dew, scattered over her body hid the hole to her heart.

It was a May of unusual beauty that year. A May unlike any other.

In the Name of Maria

One procession for Non di Maria, the Virgin Mary's name day, comes to mind. The year Maria Cosaria and Vico da Ùa broke up. Now, well before they even counted eighteen years they set eyes on each other. Took some time, but Vico got a job at the brick factory, gave Maria a big flashy ring. Looked like a chunk of glass you'd find on the road—maybe an accident, a piece of somebody's windshield, so big it was.

For a good while that big ring tied them together, then Maria and Vico had one of those fights over nothing that winds up being everything. Vico wanted his ring back. Natural, that. Probably pledged plenty of wages not yet earned to buy it. But Maria said, after all their time together, he owed her that ring. He said, since she didn't want him she shouldn't want his goods either, their attachment being over. So mad they were they got go-betweens—sworn to highest secrecy, you understand—to relay messages.

Back and forth the recriminations traveled. Time soon ate away the seal on the go-betweens' lips. And unbeknownst to the other, each repeated the secret messages to one, and only one, true friend who, of course, swore never, *never*, to repeat a word. You can imagine. Faster than Satan's pitchfork stabbing a sinner, the whole village knew.

And Vico's mother! Maria's! You should have heard. Better than any politician, they were, drumming up support for her own. Village split into camps, hurled insults

9

at the other side. Maria's money hungry. Vico's cheap. She's a liar! He's untrue!

Now, Maria Cosaria was angry. She didn't want to give that ring back. If she did, it was as good as saying she was wrong. But keeping it branded her as greedy and grasping. There she was, unmarried, with no prospects in sight—most men her age having already gone to the altar, and those who hadn't, didn't for a good reason—but even among them, her worth would suffer if she kept the ring.

All this was going on near the time of Non di Maria. September. Fields are rich, giving their best. Grapes beginning to swell, plums and pears pulling branches low, bees buzzing all around, cinquantina corn standing tall—came from Wisconsin, those seeds did. So good, this season.

That Sunday the bells announced the procession was leaving the church, same as always. First came the altar boys, then little girl angels with baskets of rose petals, the almost-ripe girls with ribbon bouquets, and the virgins in white holding fancy pillows with offerings.

Now these signorine got all the attention, not just from the bachelors, but the entire village because of the pillows they carried on outstretched arms. Everyone wanted to see who offered what to the Blessed Virgin in thanks or in supplication: a homemade lace heart, a hand embroidered handkerchief, maybe a store-bought medallion. All given to the Madonna, then displayed in church for everyone to see.

Like always, the procession started at the head of the village near where Maria Cosaria lived. She came out, her hand moved fast over the Madonna's blue pillow trimmed in gold.

Slow, the procession made its way. More and more villagers started walking alongside the closer the procession got to Vico da Ùa's house. Vico's mother, a tree stump of a woman with a lip shaded by an umbrella of hair, watched from the door. She had campaigned hard, lashing her tongue across the village: her Vico was hard working, honest, good looking, and that two-faced Maria was just a money grubbing good-for-nothing.

Something on the cushion caught the light, winked at the mother. She shouldered into the crowd. She stared. She screamed.

Vico rushed to his mother's side. He squinted, tilted his head like the sun was burning his eyes. He tried to pick up what was sewn onto the pillow so tight the material was puckered and dirtied from fondling. A wail rose to heaven. Madonna! Madonna! His mother clutched her breast.

There was nothing Vico da Ùa could do. Not with the ring, his ring to Maria Cosaria, going to the Virgin Mary.

La Fuessa

It happened in summer. It happened when clusters of new grapes weighted vines of laced leaves and sun ripened the earth.

It happened on a day Meni Mulinar looped his shoulders into the leather straps of a brass canister, sprayhose in his hand. One pocket of his jacket sagged with crystals of copper sulfate to make verderame for the vines; the other held his reward, a half-cigar, and boxed matchsticks to light it. Celestina carried Fausto, the beloved son, the only one of three to survive. Delia, the firstborn, carried empty baskets hooked on each thin arm.

Under radiant light the three trudged to Il Ronc, the far hillside granted to the Mulinar to till as their own by the landowner. On that productive patch tilted to sunlight all the day, grapes grew that would weight Meni's pockets with money for seed, Sunday bread and Sunday shoes. Money too soon a memory once the dry grocer and seed store were paid and too much spent at the osteria to buy back the wine his grapes had made.

That day, the three passed the fuessa, a shadowed pool fed by spring rains and summer downpours. From that stony hollow nestled in the hill, stagnant water helped the Mulinar tend their vineyard.

On Il Ronc's stippled slope Celestina spread Meni's jacket beneath sheltering tree branches, lay Fausto down to nap. Meni broke a shield of slime to dip the brass container into the fuessa. Mosquitoes and dragonflies clouded Meni's face and hands. The water within the brass container blossomed into blue verderame as copper sulfate crystals dissolved.

Back and forth between lines of vines Meni pumped verderame. The clear blue solution stained the broad grape leaves gray. Celestina bent low over rows of zucchini planted between grapevines bound to wire. With both hands Delia carried baskets of squash to row's end.

The sun rose to the zenith. The earth exhaled heat into light. Cicadas strummed in song. Perspiration pebbled brows.

The sound rising in the still air was unlike any the Mulinar had ever heard. They looked to where it came. They saw a flaming bundle beneath a wide branching tree. A high pitched shriek sent them racing. The brass canister thudded to the ground spilling verderame, a fallen basket spewed green zucchini. A chorus of cries rose shimmering against blind sun.

Meni snatched his burning son, threw him into the fuessa. Cicadas shrilled. The last of the matches floated from Fausto's slack fingers. Celestina stamped a bare foot against the burning jacket, stripped off her underskirt to wrap the raw body of her only son. Meni, running across green hill and green field, carried his screaming child to the nearest farmhouse. Astride a borrowed horse he raced to the village doctor. The man looked at the body bundled in fine white, kept his hands at his side. "Take him home. Let him die there."

Don Fiore walked to the mill on the Viarsa, anointed Fausto's blistered forehead. Spasms and cries answered the priest's touch. He trudged toward the little bridge to the village hearing the hammer of fate and failure in his ears.

The cicadas rasped. Dark flecks littered white sheets. Each day Celestina changed the bed linens, making sure her son would have a worthy shroud. A gauze net draped the small bed, black flies circled above. A fan of woven cornleaves fluttered in midday heat. Celestina crooned a tuneless lullaby. Meni stood at his son's feet, Angelus bells rang over the hills. Delia, silent and close, kept mother and brother company. At bedtime Celestina sat near, rosary beads sifting through tired fingers, keeping time to whimpers of pain.

One morning, Fausto spoke a word no one knew. A name, it seemed. He repeated it when Don Fiore came to console and comfort. The priest, consoled and comforted, hurried to the village.

The scent of rain promised relief, a change, when Don Fiore greeted Celestina once again and nodded to Delia, her lap filled with beans, a basket of pink and white pods at her feet.

Eyes bright with hope, the priest stood over Fausto, eyes sealed against the light. With a murmured prayer Don Fiore splashed water from a distant place over the burned boy.

Oddly, the child did not scream at its touch. Oddly, the child's cries quieted as one season edged into another. Oddly, when the cicadas chorused in the months of heat in the following year, Meni with his brass canister for verderame on his back, Celestina with empty baskets dangling from each arm, and Delia holding her brother Fausto by the hand walked past the fuessa in the vineyard on the hill known as Il Ronc.

That water brought from a place the priest had only

heard named, a faraway place named Lourdes, was the Madonna's gift to the Mulinar.

Villagers called it a miracle. They still do to this day.

Rabbit Hole

George Lemain stood above the prone brunette, her long hair fallen loose across her cheek, arm thrown out, white satchel nearby. Pity, he said to himself, lifting limp brown strands. The neat line in her neck might have passed as a wrinkle the sun missed tanning except for the clotted blood.

Pity, George said again. Forty-one days from retiring and a dead body on the beach. A foreign dead body. He narrowed pale eyes, skimmed the turquoise waters kissing the white sands of Cloister Cove favored by honeymooners and weekend sailors, surveyed fishing boats and clipper ships strung across the sea.

George turned the key in the ignition. The coroner would make her presentable for those who had accompanied her to her fate. His own fate unfolded as straight and unchecked as the blacktop back to Harbor Town.

The clipped menace in the Commissioner's cold voice underscored the need for speed, first to rein in bad publicity in this time of faltering tourism, then to identify a killer. Any killer, George amended silently. What a career capstone, continued the Commissioner, if you should quickly capture the culprit. Surely, after salvaging the island's reputation as the jewel of the Caribbean, George could be granted a delayed, but decidedly deserved, salary increase, boosting his retirement income from modest to generous.

That conversation prompted George to Horatio's Café. Jack Cabot made a point of catering to tourist ideas of an exotic and exciting past of what once was a backwater until affluence and ennui discovered the island. Jack's café reeked of the ersatz. But he could also provide the unadulterated and hard to get.

"Bad for business, Inspector." Jack carried a coffee cup to George's table, pulled up a chair.

George sipped the brew, swallowed only after the tingling subsided. The liquid was almost as smooth as Jack himself, an outsider who managed to infiltrate the island's workings with the ease and anonymity of a local. Up to a point. George knew about Jack's stash in the back room. "Poor girl."

"She wanted to shake family, wandered off alone maybe to have a little adventure. Nothing new."

"She's dead. The Commissioner is upset." George gripped the cup with bony fingers. "There were five fishing boats within range of the crime scene. I should think there were as many or more earlier. Perhaps, someone saw something. Fishermen are a keen eyed lot."

"Depends," Jack offered more of his special brew. "Busy fishing or busy watching?"

"Or watching to make a catch. Earn a little something extra. Talk travels."

"Only so far."

"Perhaps." George checked his watch. "I must get to the office." He met Jack's wary eye. "By the way, wasn't that your friend Pablo's boat at Pearl Point last night? The full moon is particularly lovely from the headlands."

Faint as the flicker was, George glimpsed it in Jack's steady gaze. George suppressed a smile, his wild shot struck home. Jack shrugged, "Talk can cost."

"Or pay off."

"Right."

George searched the terse blue line stretched across his office window. The past three days had been busy with bar brawls and knife fights. The stunned family told what little they knew, identified the satchel contents, asked for her body. George kept the digital camera.

He exercised patience. Soon he was rewarded. Taciturn, sturdy shouldered, well muscled Morris Tisan, 24, itinerant fisherman from Nevis, led him to his ramshackle hut under trees near the bluegreen sea. George opened a drawer, held up a silver box. Tisan's dark eyes darted from the digital camera to the Inspector's conspiratorial smile. Tisan confessed.

"The Commissioner was most pleased, Jack. Swift solution to a publicity nightmare, law and order prevail, tourists may once again frolic mindlessly." George massaged the tingling liquid with a slow tongue. "Unsurpassed, Cuban rum."

"Private reserve, best enjoyed in private." Jack unlatched a small wooden box. "Try one."

George held up his hand, "I don't smoke cigars, Cuban or otherwise." He rose. "It is good of you to invite me to the back room."

"Come again, come often."

George blinked at sudden sunlight. "Incidentally, Pablo should have no problem delivering your supplies in the near term, and I'll do my best to ensure that remains so afterwards. Twenty-nine days to retirement."

Jack clapped George's back, walked him to the car.

George switched on the ignition. "By the way, the Commissioner intends to play to the media and ask for the death penalty. Tell Tisan not to worry. Assure him the money arrived in Nevis, his mother is well."

FENG SHUI

She watched the old man looking out the window. His hand rested in the sunlight on the chair arm. His cane, black and shiny, rested beside him. He was waiting. Hands at her sides, she stood in kitchen shadow, watching and waiting with him.

It hadn't always been so. They believed. Threw their energy, their savings into one last effort. We can make a go of it they told each other. The fortunetellers, all three, assured them. The feng shui of the place they found was favorable, wind and water in balance, proper for their endeavor. The door was positioned for luck to enter. So she and the old man signed the lease for the place they found, a big space not far from the El station that brought workers walking past their restaurant door.

The fortunetellers foresaw well. Bustle and noise filled the place they found, sounded of hope, of possibility. Success. They greeted people, darted among tables, worked for a comfortable old age. But the luck entering their door changed. Fewer took the El to work, fewer walked through their door. Still, she and the old man stayed, hoped, until the place they found sucked the life from them.

She touched the table, the one she salvaged from their old home. It was too large for this space, but it comforted them both. The table was shiny and smooth, familiar. A frypan was ready on the stove, a platter of chopped vegetables and sliced pork balanced on the tiny counter. She would cook the old man his favorite dish once their waiting was over.

"It is the life. The one we must live," she murmured. She knew the old man would not hear her words, his ears already closing out the sounds of life. The phone had rung too many times to tell them of a friend's passing, so he stopped hearing the ring of remembrance. He was lonely she knew. "I do my best, try to make it easy," she told him when the silence grew too great. "I cannot do everything. You must try, try to be yourself." But he grew lost to himself.

The old man's hand stretched into the light, he stood, wavering. She moved to his side. Together, they watched a pair of ducks glide on a pale band of yellow and slip soundlessly into a pool of blue water. She touched the old man's hand, soft and smooth as a child's.

The male with its gleaming green head swam purposefully, his mate at his side. A soft wind tickled the face of the water, lifted the pair into the brightness beyond.

The Little Chair

When I was little my big brother came home with a rocking chair just my size and put it down near the coal stove in the big room. The chair was chubby and cute, the wood colored like ruddy cheeks. Three round fingers of wood fanned up to hold the back panel, curved like a smile. The end of the arms, resting on rounded posts pegged into the seat, curled into just the right size for my hands to hold. I rocked in it when the back room where the family lived was noisy and busy. I rocked in it when it was quiet and dark, my mother fixing hair in the beauty parlor up front or lying down on the big bed we shared.

My big sister, the one next to me in line, came home with a decal. She asked if I wanted it on the little chair. I nodded yes. So she centered the decal in the middle of the back panel and peeled away the clear cover to leave behind flowers in quiet red, yellow and green.

One day I leaned back to rock and heard a crack. One of the curved shoes the rocker wore broke and left the little chair hobbled. My sisters tried to put it back together, but couldn't. When my big brother came over for dinner, he carried the rocker out to the backyard. In his right hand he held the crowbar, hammer and saw, the tools he used to break down shipping crates into wood for the coal stove. He came back inside and set down a little chair that stood still on four legs instead of rocking

Later, one of the arms wobbled, then let go of the chair. The next time my brother came home he took the one-armed chair outside. It came back with no arms at all. Then the little chair was handy for anyone to use.

I stood on it to reach the kitchen sink when I washed rice until I didn't need it anymore. Then it stayed by the white water heater. Get me the little chair my mother would say when she needed to reach up and get the dishes we used for special occasions.

The ruddy red wood faded and the decal lost luster. But when we moved from the old house to an apartment with a real kitchen and windows without bars, the chair came with us. It stood next to the white rice box my brother built in woodworking shop a long long time before. The little chair was handy and fit in anywhere so it came along when my mother got her dream house, then on to the condo.

There, it stood sentry by the entryway. My mother rested her pocketbook on the little chair while she put on her coat. Her handbag got bigger and heavier as she grew thinner and smaller, the number of purse compartments, pockets and pouches growing as she grew older. In those small spaces she kept things separate and easy for her to find and hard for thieves to steal.

Now, my sister, the one next to me in line, keeps the little chair tucked out of the way. She's the only one who still lives near where the family used to live. She stores the black treadle Singer sewing machine and the better odds and ends my mother thought might come in handy. My sister's kids are grown up and have kids of their own. Her oldest daughter is hoping for her first grandchild. Every time my niece visits my sister's house, she sees that little chair sitting quietly in the corner. She runs her hand across the front of the chair back to feel the last pieces of the decal that go all the way back to the old house in Chinatown. It tells a story, that little chair, a story about us. About family.

How Come

You ask me how come. How come I keep renewing my beauty certificate. Haven't fixed hair in a long long time. Too old. But I like it, the idea. Reminds me of lots of things.

Fifth grade. That's all the schooling I got. Was the oldest one in class back in Cleveland, they laughed at me. I told Foster Mother I didn't want to go back. She said I didn't have to. The Truant Officer came, she played dumb, no speak-ee English.

Foster Mother never wanted to come to Gold Mountain, you know, America. But Foster Father insisted. He wanted the family together, have her and their grown son with him. But she didn't want to leave the life she knew, be all alone in a strange place. So he told her she could take someone with her to keep her company. That's why she bought me.

My Auntie took me around to all the big houses trying to sell me. I was eight. Foster Mother asked Auntie and me a few questions, then told us to come back. Next time, Foster Mother left me alone in a room. There was a toy on the table. A wooden puzzle all in pieces. I put it together. It was a little round mouse. Foster Mother was watching but I didn't know it. She asked if I would like to come again. I said yes. I got to know her, see her way of living. One day Auntie brought me there, told me she would come for me later. I knew she wouldn't.

My father came to visit, asked how I liked it. Sometimes I watched for him at the window, looked for him on the

24

road carrying things to market. I would go down to the gate to talk to him. My ma came once. She brought my little sister, that made me real happy. I used to take care of her, and I was so glad to play with her again. She was just beginning to walk when they sold me. My ma was wearing a new dress. I touched her knee, brushed my hand over the silk. Smooth, soft, so beautiful. Oh, so beautiful!

Foster Mother was good to me. You remember that picture of me and my foster family? I'm sitting on a chair that's too big. My feet dangling above the floor. I'm the only one wearing leather shoes, everybody else had cloth ones, even their son. Cost money, leather shoes. And the neck ring I had—those days, girls wore a collar of twisted metal—was of silver, not some cheap stuff like most.

When I got sold I didn't know about America. So when Foster Mother told me we were leaving for Gold Mountain I asked her. Asked her if I could go home, say goodbye to my ma. Foster Mother said no.

The boat trip was long, weeks and weeks. I cried myself to sleep thinking about my family. It was far, so far I could never go back. Never see my ma again, my little sister. I cried and cried. Told myself to forget. Forget all about them. How many brothers and sisters I had, their names, their ages. Forget my father's name, the name of my village.

It took a long time, but I forgot. Forgot everything. Forgot for good.

Foster Father was a big shot, owned restaurants in Cleveland. We lived in a big fancy house in a nice part of town. Trees and gardens. Foster Mother let me have a bedroom all to myself. The only one with a balcony, like a princess. There was lots of coming and going at the house.

People coming to pay respect to Foster Father. Maybe ask for a favor. Get help.

Like your Daddy. He was looking for a second wife but I didn't know that when Foster Father introduced him to me. Daddy was 28, owned a restaurant in Lansing. He came to the house a few times, we talked. His way of speaking, his manners, how he handled himself was nice. Refined.

After one of Daddy's visits, Foster Mother took me aside, asked if I liked him. He wanted to marry me. I didn't know what to say. I asked her, asked Foster Mother what I should do. I cannot tell you she said. It is for you to decide. She asked again if I liked him. She wanted me to be sure. Said it was for the rest of my life.

The matchmaker came. Daddy and I got married. I was 14.

Daddy told me his parents sent him to school in Macao. Then they told him to come back. Come back to get married. They chose a village girl for him. He didn't like village life. He didn't like his wife.

A hick, that's what he called her. Dressed like one, too. Didn't want to be seen riding with her through the village so he got out of the carriage and walked to the New Year feast. Their first child was a girl. So was the second. Daddy's mother screamed smother her, smother her! Daddy was disgusted but said, oh, let her live. Then he left for good. Left for Gold Mountain. Started out in Oakland working for someone else, then moved to Lansing, opened his own place. Things were good back in the early '20s.

My firstborn was a boy. I was so happy. So proud. My foster parents came to Lansing for his Month Old party.

As soon as I could, I had a picture of him taken to send back to Daddy's first wife. To show her my respect, to let her know the family name would continue. My second-born was also a boy. I couldn't believe my luck.

But things started to change. It was 1929. Foster Mother paid me a visit. We lived in Jackson then. I told her Daddy was having a hard time making a go of it. No matter how he tried, he had no success. I said maybe it was me, my life was unlucky. No, she said, it is not you. It is your husband. His life is unlucky.

The Depression, then the war. We quit moving. Daddy was sick by then. I had six kids, four of them girls, all of them too young to know any better. I had to do something. So I went to beauty school. The women in Chinatown talked. Me, leaving my kids to take care of each other, going downtown, doing something on my own.

At beauty school they asked if I had a high school diploma. They said I couldn't get a license to fix hair without one. I explained to them why I wanted to be a beautician, my kids, my husband too sick to work. One of the teachers understood, a white lady. She helped me after class to learn the things I needed to know for the high school test. I passed. I got my license. When it arrived I jumped up and down, I was so excited. I opened the beauty parlor. Then Daddy died.

I kept the family together. That beauty license hanging on the wall reminds me. My life. You kids, married, making your own life. Then I got to thinking. Thinking maybe I could go back to China, find out what happened to my little sister, my brothers. Maybe they're even somewhere in the US.

That's how come I went back to Cleveland. Remember, last spring? Made a special trip to the old neighborhood to see my sister-in-law, the wife of my foster brother. She was sick, real sick. I explained to her I wanted to go home. Told her I couldn't remember the name of my father or his village. She was the only one alive who knew, knew about me, where I'm from. We are both old I said. Everyone else is gone, there would be no disrespect if you tell me.

My sister-in-law thought about it a long long time. Then she said she couldn't, couldn't break her word. Foster Mother made her promise before dying, made my sister-in-law promise never to tell me. Foster Mother still kept me from going home, finding out who I really was. I was very disappointed.

The Chinese have a saying. Your life is made before you.

Rat Race

Back when the world was as large as a room at the end of a long hall, life was simple. In that womb of a room on a night in early June, three of a family of seven—a trio of females ages apart—shared chills and thrills.

The girl worked on her homework at the dining table while her little sister, kneeling on a chair across from her, scribbled crayon all over a clown outlined in black. The mother screamed. Even for this family still unsettled by the death of father and husband that cry in the night startled.

The girl jumped to her feet. "Ma, what's the matter?"

"A rat!"

The girl dashed toward the bedroom. She spotted beady eyes staring at her. She screamed. The black and white rat skittered into the shadowy hall. Then the mother shot out into the big room where the family's living was done.

Safe at the big table bright under a bare bulb, the little sister watched, curious. She'd seen rats before, but never her mother and sister running around screaming their heads off.

Scared by the long dark hallway the rat reversed, headed for the light. The girl saw it coming, jumped aside. Hollering to high heaven, she grabbed the pocket handles on each side of the sliding bathroom door, hoisted both feet up off the floor.

The rat raced past her into the big room. The mother screamed, beat linoleum with slippered feet, waved her hands, yelled to make the rat backtrack down the hall to the beauty parlor where she fixed hair.

The little sister marveled in silence, her big sister still kept her legs way up in the air.

Seeing flailing legs and flapping arms, the scared rat darted under the davenport.

"Get it!" the mother yelled over her shoulder, running fast past the big table.

The girl leapt from bathroom to potbellied stove, picked up coal shovel and scuttle, banged them together.

At the barred back door, the mother lifted the two-by-four from metal brackets screwed into the doorframe. The girl kept clanging away.

Desperate eyes peered from under the maroon davenport. The rat inched back from the racket.

The mother unhooked the screen door, unbolted the outside entrance to the yard of weeds shared by three flats. Holding screen in one hand and yard door in the other, she yelled, "Chase it out this way!" Her pajamas and housecoat filled a slit of space between the two doors.

The girl crept closer to the davenport, sweeping the coal shovel side to side.

Frightened, the rat scuttled out. The girl screamed, dropped pail and spade. A black and white blur bolted past the big table. The little sister noticed the rat's long and scraggly hair, twisted around to follow it to the door.

The rat balked, stopped dead in its tracks right in front of the mother. She screamed. Confused, the rat spun around. The mother, beating a tattoo with her feet between the open doors, screeched, "Do something!"

The girl rattled shovel inside scuttle, inched forward. Confronted, the black and white rat turned tail, ran into the quiet starry night.

The little sister sat back on her heels. Life went back to being simple.

Standard Procedure

"Dead? What do you mean dead?"

"Dead, as in deceased." Cassandra shivered. Look at those eyes of Jennifer's going into night light mode like a cat's, all yellow flecks.

The surprise of Ms. Seen-It-All Jennifer, the handler of Hires and Fires, was one of the many surprises that eventful day in September. One of the strange but true incidents in the life of Cassandra Hardy, admin. One of thousands at desks in corporations helmed by CEOs and presidents, buttressed by executives who execute (sometimes terminally) and line management who manage a line of titled, semi-titled, and non-titled variously recompensed employees. The juggernaut of America's business stolidly moving forward into the worldwide arena. And there Cassandra was, a cog within a wheel within a wheel running from 8:00 to 5:00 Monday through Friday, a good gerbil in her cube scrambling through paper piles as fast as she could. In other words, another grunt in the war on making a living.

"We just hired him!" Jennifer sagged against the cubicle, the wall panel shook.

That shook Cassandra. Jennifer was never left without words. What if she passed out? Or puked!

"He's been here ten days, not long enough to make enemies," Jennifer mumbled.

"He was a nice guy. He actually came around to meet me, an admin. That was a first."

"How do you know, dead?" Jennifer was getting to be her old self again.

Cassandra whispered the facts, just the facts, she'd been given. The new exec woke up dead. Worse, he didn't show for a meeting with the new head honchos, Mutt and Jeff.

The twosome had descended from on high, that is, the Board of Directors. New blood and outsider know-how was the best bet to get the earnings up off the floor and into the stratosphere. The Board decided a two-for-one team would not only double company expenses, but also double company income. You have to spend money to make money.

Paying for the second chief exec triggered a Reduction in Force. The workload of the RIFed employees fell on the shoulders of the survivors at no additional cost due to an immediate salary freeze with increased production per grunt without further investment, thanks to an immediate hiring freeze.

The anointed pair trimmed titles and payroll further by combining the sales and marketing departments under the new guy: the not-yet-dead exec. Hiring him rendered two company veterans redundant. Each walked out the door, separation package in hand: money and perks to soothe ego and expenses until the next title came along. Restructuring, top to bottom, the ideal business model.

The lame duck department heads made nice with the chosen company saviors. Those answering to the lame ducks hid fears of cuts and slashes in personnel and budget behind hosannas voiced with false enthusiasm and crossed fingers.

"How could he be dead?"

"How should I know? My hotline to heaven's down, mainframe problems." Sarcasm was second nature to

Cassandra. It kept her safe among rank and file. She formed the weaker half of the Dreaded Duo. Jennifer held more clout. She occupied the smallest and most crammed office in the department, but it had a door and a sliver of window. Line management knew never to cross the line with Jennifer Ricketts.

"He was pretty young. Looked healthy, in shape. What about the execs? How did they take it?"

"Not personally. They gave the guy the benefit of the doubt. Two weeks was too soon for insubordination, so they waited. After an hour they got worried. Late is one thing, no-show is another. They got Dolores to call the hotel. The maid found him in bed. Dead."

Jennifer's cat eyes flickered. "Not good."

"Dolores called me asking if I could find out the wife's name without explaining why. An odd question, even for Dolores, but who am I to question the exec assistant? Checked the new guy's resume, no spouse named. Why should he? We hired him, not his wife and kids."

Jennifer's synapses were sizzling again. "Did you tell Maggie?"

"Didn't know if I should. Confidentiality. You know how fast scuttlebutt travels. Can't you hear the company wise guys: See, working here can kill you.

"But Maggie's got to know. She's got to delete him from the system. Medical, dental."

"Why? The guy's not going to file any claims."

"But the next of kin might. Death benefits."

"Ooh, no wonder the big deal about the wife. Mutt and Jeff probably wanted to delegate someone to call her. Can you imagine?" Cassandra dropped her voice. "We're sorry to inform you, but you're a widow. We were pleased to have your husband join our team, brief as his tenure was."

Jennifer straightened her shoulders, marched toward her office. "I better start the paperwork, make sure Maggie gets me the backup on his health plan."

The phone rang. It was Dolores. Mutt and Jeff wanted Cassandra to draft an announcement about the dead executive. They were going company-wide but keeping it out of the newspapers.

It was busy. A reporter pounded on the locked foyer door at 4:30. Nobody answered the doorbell to the Executive Offices he told Cassandra. No, she couldn't let him in, she was only an admin. No, she couldn't tell him anything about the deceased. The reporter took the express elevator to the lobby.

"We made it." Jennifer leaned on Cassandra's cubicle. They were the only ones left, everybody else rushed the exits at the stroke of 5:00.

"So, who got stuck calling the dead exec's wife?" Cassandra locked up.

"No one. Our coroner called their coroner. Mutt and Jeff got off the hook."

"The pecking order comes to the rescue once again." Cassandra started for the door. "Standard procedure. Like always."

SHANA AND CORBIN

You know what Shana says. Disabled. But I don't believe it. Corbin's sly. I mean, you have to be to play Shana's game and win. Far as I can tell, Corbin gets his way. What kills me is how he does it. Doesn't open his mouth. Not that I don't know what his voice sounds like. Corbin only exercises his vocal chords when Shana isn't around. Twenty-six years of watching taught Corbin how to handle his mama.

Take dinner. Shana's rampaging through the kitchen banging pans like a banshee. Doesn't bother Corbin one bit, not just because he's lying down in his bedroom but also because he's got his hearing aids turned off. Shana doesn't know it, but Corbin knows it, and I know it. We both know what Shana's doing. But Corbin and me aren't buying it. No siree. We're not about to light any candles in front of Saint Shana.

Now, Corbin knows, and I know, that if we so much as cast a shadow on the holy mess in the kitchen and try to help, Shana would give us That Look. Those purple irises of hers flash enough heat to sizzle bacon. Warn us to stay out, the only thing you can do is damage.

Corbin knows what he's not hearing, just like he knows when to come to the dining room. Precisely at 6:23 the table will be set for him, like it should be. He knows Shana knows he's disabled. She told him so all his life.

You probably think Corbin's some kind of drab moth pinned to Shana's conscience, but, like I said, Corbin is cunning. He lets Shana think she talked him into going to the adult center. But I know Corbin knows the reason why he's up on his own and dressed by 9:00 every weekday. Corbin, with his broad shoulders and tousled tawny hair, is getting his chance.

Corbin likes women. Even Shana knows that from their strolls down the main drag. They make a peculiar pair. Him head and shoulders taller and lots thinner than her. Her ogling shop displays, rattling on about a dream vacation in front of windows plastered with posters of palm trees. Him ogling the women walking his way. Whenever Corbin spots a girl with the looks he likes he lifts his right hand to heart level and wags it back and forth like a windshield wiper. That's what Shana says and what I see. Some girls reward him with a smile, some stalk past, rigid on the road to salvation. He's just friendly is how Shana explains that wagging hand. Right, I say, giving Corbin an eyeball kiss. He knows what's up, and so do I.

The care center is something else. Rife with females. All ages and sizes of mind. I notice, Shana notices and Corbin notices when we bring him the first day. A female, somewhere between the ages of 19 and 69, with a gimpy eye and a limp leg zeroes in on the tall specimen with the short mother and strange friend when we walk in. She wraps Corbin's hand in a death grip, pulls him away. Her eye wasn't the only thing that strayed, it turns out.

Nothing to worry about, the counselor counsels Shana once we find them. Shana looks at Corbin's blank face, believes what she hears. I look behind those empty eyes and see what he's up to. Corbin the Cunning playing innocent.

Corbin learns to read out loud, parsing the syllables like dimes dropped one by one into the till, and write. Corbin writes when he sits at the short sofa shoved against the wall behind the dining table. Loud and clear he prints: Andy is an asshole.

Shana tells me Corbin doesn't know what the words mean. He just repeats in writing what he hears filtered through hearing aids. I know he knows what he means. It's Shana who doesn't know what he means. Shana, who owns every key and turns every knob, is the stranger in this house.

Corbin writes when Shana is off schedule, like she is to-night. The smell of burn sneaks from the kitchen chased by a splatter of swear words chopped short by the exhaust fan. Shana glares a warning to my mouth, hanging open like it usually does when it comes to her. I'm not quite family and I'm more than a friend, but not much more. I'm Corbin's voice, so to speak, and I usually don't. Zip my mouth, mind my manners. Corbin's a good teacher, yes siree.

Sometimes he eludes me. I suspect escapades. Not like Shana, who expects what she wants. She says Corbin doesn't understand real life. Corbin's disabled. He doesn't look disabled when he steps out of the shower, not that I get a look-see on a regular basis, but I believe my eyes more than her words. And he sure isn't handicapped handling the trainee with long hair straight as wheat. I catch the act because Shana sent me early to get him. There he is, sidling up close, I forget her name but I recognize parts of her. He smiles, she smiles. She turns to pick up a notebook, his hand shoots out to get it for her, grazes her pet-me-pretty-please breast. She looks at him, her mouth wrestling with how to respond. He looks vacant but leaves his hand on her cleavage. She smiles, says something I can't hear, steps back. He smiles, lifts his hand to his heart and waves three short strokes. I grin. Corbin, the con man.

I wonder what he's thinking when I go to get him for dinner at 6:20. He's lying down, one eye on the clock, the other on a cobweb covering a ceiling crack. It's too early, but Shana's on a roll and wants to test a new recipe on us pronto. From the way Corbin pushes his lower lip into a wet pout I know he's concentrating on something. I figure it's the trainee with the wheat hair and the firm boobs. The more I watch him stretched on that bed, late sun gilding his face like some exotic god, I think he's thinking about plowing a wheat field. My thinking this makes me wonder.

Corbin doesn't get up from bed until the big hand's on 6:00 and the little one creeps to 23. Shana, wearing an apron splashed with red, plants a platter of something unidentifiable puddled in sauce on the table. Corbin takes one look, heads to his room. A hail of words hard as rocks bounce off his back. Shana revs up for round two but Corbin returns, bypasses the table for the sofa. Shana gathers fire to shoot a look hot enough to scorch skin. Corbin, the sly guy, moves quick. A pair of dead black sunglasses hit his nose and hide his eyes in a move as smooth as him copping a feel. Behind the shades his eyes must be laughing. Then he sits down, crosses his legs.

I almost choke swallowing the snicker tickling my throat. Corbin, one. Shana, zee-ro.

By the time Shana's put something recognizable on the table Corbin's printed a few neat rows of square letters: Andy is an asshole. Catherine is sweet. I like sweet. I eat sweet.

Nope. Nothing disabled about Corbin.

Killer Lips

Dahlia Livingston and Mildred Trusdale sat at a window table. Dahlia licked her lips of champagne, watched the waiter walk away. "Very nice."

"What?" Dred eyed her old high school friend.

"The champagne, of course." Dahlia's laugh tinkled in the empty dining room. "Sure you won't have some, just to whet the appetite?"

Before Dred could answer, Dahlia raised her red tipped fingers and arched a perfectly shaped eyebrow. The young man, dark and handsome, swept back to their table.

Dahlia flashed a radiant smile. "Another glass of champagne, please."

"Of course." The waiter moved away with grace.

Dahlia leaned across the butter plate, "He's cute!"

"Give him a break, Dahlia, he's only a kid trying to make a living."

"Why, whatever do you mean, Dred? He must be 25 at least."

"A baby in swaddling clothing."

Outside, a streetcar scooted around the corner clanging at a jaywalking tourist and catching Dahlia's attention. "Must be new. There weren't any streetcars when I lived here."

"Well, that was way back in the heyday of free love. By the way, how come you weren't willing to visit your old stomping grounds until now?"

"Who wants to go back to the scene of the crime."

"Crime, what crime?"

A thin flute of pale champagne descended in front of Dred's eyes.

"Are you ready for me or do you want a few minutes?" The waiter bowed to one, then the other.

Dahlia looked into his coffee-dark eyes, her smile widened as she took in his straight nose and square jaw. "Oh, we need some time together," she breathed.

"Certainly, take whatever you need." He slipped soundlessly into a sea of white tablecloths.

Dahlia lifted her glass, "To us! Let the next grand adventure begin!"

"Right, to the challenges ahead." Bubbles tickled Dred's nose.

"Challenges? Come on, Dred, what challenges? There's nothing we can't handle. Been there, done that."

"You think so?" Dred swallowed a burp. "We're heading into unknown territory: middle age, the vast featureless plain between youth and senility."

"Don't be such a pessimist! Think of it this way, now we can afford what we want. Might as well enjoy it. Drink up!"

A slow stream of suits started sitting down at the tables surrounding them.

"We better order, the place is filling up." Dred scanned the list of italics printed on ecru. "What are you going to get?"

Dahlia cast a fetching smile at their young and handsome waiter, who backtracked to their table. She tapped a red fingertip against the wine list, "We'll take a bottle of Robert Mondaví."

Dahlia pronounced the vintner's name with a French flair, knocking off the *t* of Robert and tipping high the *i* of Mondavi. Young and Handsome never flinched, but held his bow until Dred repeated Robert Mondavi in her unmistakable Midwestern accent. He floated away with a nod to each of them.

"Remember you're back in the States, Dahlia, blend in with the locals and speak their language. And remember that confession is good for the soul. Let's hear about the crime."

Dahlia's red fingernails fanned out on the menu, a gold tassel dangled in the center crease. "A youthful indiscretion, that's all. The goat cheese and frisée salad sounds scrumptious."

"Youthful indiscretion? That's no crime. Your teens were a string of them. I'm leaning toward the bisque."

A cork popped. A ruby red rivulet shimmied into a goblet. Dahlia Livingston laced her fingers under the glass, swirled, sniffed, and sipped. She carefully massaged the wine with her tongue before swallowing. Dahlia lifted her face of peaches and cream—the best money could buy—and pressed her cherry lips into a slow smile. "Good," she cooed to Young and Handsome. He smiled, poured, and retreated.

"Bisque brings back bad memories."

"Don't tell me you barfed."

"Don't be so graphic, Mildred! It was a killer meal."

"Oh, you cooked."

"No, Jonathan did. It was awful."

"I never ate a meal of Jonathan's I didn't like."

"It wasn't his cooking, it's what happened at the table. Thank goodness I had the presence of mind to call the ambulance and fill out the police report." Dahlia fixed her chocolate bon-bon eyes on Dred's alarmed blue ones. "Of course, what happened at dinner wasn't half as bad as what happened when I lived out here."

"Ladies," a velvet voice asked, "are you ready?" Young and Handsome hovered.

"Oh, yes." Dahlia dimpled a smile at him. "Yes, I'm ready."

He smiled, she smiled. He dropped an inch closer. Dred coughed. His head shot to her.

"Seems my friend's still mulling things over, so I'll have the bisque and...."

"Are you sure, Dred? Goat cheese is very good." Dahlia darted a laughing smile at Young and Handsome, "We'll both have the frisée and goat cheese salad. No caramel-ized walnuts for me."

"Put them on mine. I want lots of everything."

Dahlia folded her menu, "And we'll order the main course later."

"Very good." Young and Handsome slipped between tables of suits.

"So, are you going to tell me?"

"You probably never had goat cheese. It's very tasty, you'll like it."

"Goat cheese I've had, but lobster bisque I haven't." Dred gulped a swallow of red. "And I haven't heard about what's worse than shipping a dinner guest off to Emergency."

Dahlia glanced around the room. The suits were talking business, the staff was serving, the tourists were staring. Dahlia lowered her head and confided, "It involved a man."

"Big deal. All your adventures involve men."

"A dead man."

Dred choked.

Two large salads of pale frizzy leaves capped with two white chunks settled silently in front of the women. "Thank you," Dred murmured.

The stunning smile affixed to Dahlia's lips died, "Oh." It was the assistant server. She forked a bit of frisée between her ripe red lips, the tip of her tongue escaped to catch a drop of vinaigrette. "Well, I don't like to kiss and tell."

"Sure you do." Dred crammed goat cheese tangled in frisée into her mouth, chewed once, then shoved it all into her left cheek with her tongue. "So, what's the story?"

"Remember that guy I dated in senior year?"

"Of course I do. I live in the past. The older man. Your first." Dred drank thirstily.

"That's right. He graduated two years before us. Well, he heard about an opportunity out here and took it, he wanted to get out of the Midwest like most sane people do. Oh sorry, Dred. You're an exception in every respect."

Dred shrugged, shoveled more greens into her mouth, chewed like a contented cow.

"So, when I got out here I ran into him quite by chance. He helped me find a place and showed me around."

"And?"

"Well, he used to hang out at this bar. I'm really not a bar person, but, as I said, youthful indiscretion. And I like trying new things."

"Yeah, like a walk on the wild side."

"Wild side? Well, perhaps. It was the '70s, after all." Dahlia's cheeks quivered like a chipmunk's as she methodically chewed the last bit of frisée. "Anyway, I was at the bar one night having a nice chat with my friend when this absolutely drop dead gorgeous guy walked in. Muscled arms, broad shoulders, wavy hair, dazzling smile. And, *and*, he could carry on a conversation. *Witty!*" Dahlia drained her glass. "Here, let me pour."

"A heart stopping encounter, no doubt."

"Oh, he was to die for!"

"Are you ready to order the entrée now?" Young and Handsome materialized among the suits and servers.

"You're just in time," giggled Dahlia. "We were just talking about the irresistible."

He smiled bravely, his eyes wary. "We have some wonderful dishes today."

Rapt, Dahlia listened to the list of specials, pursed her lips into a strawberry kiss and shook her head. "I just can't decide between swordfish and sole." She looked him dead in the eye. "What would you take if you could have it?"

Dred coughed into her napkin.

"Are you all right?" Young and Handsome asked solicitously.

Dred nodded and guzzled water. "Yes, thank you. I know what I want, I'll go for the sole. Swordfish is too dry for me."

"An excellent choice," he beamed.

"Well, let me have the swordfish." Dahlia snapped the menu closed.

Young and Handsome bowed.

Dahlia followed his back with her eyes. "Nice. But not as nice as the fellow I was talking about." She smiled into her glass. "We got along so well!"

"At the bar or in bed?"

Dahlia's laughter soared above the clink of glasses and the clatter of silver. "He was divine! His timing was perfect until the end." She picked up the bottle, "Shall we?"

"Why not, my liver's pickled already." Dred saluted her old friend. "Cheers. Memories are made of this."

"We really should be having white with fish, but you don't do white after red."

Oversized plates with undersized servings of fish— one drenched in capers and lemon butter and the other dry and bare as the unvarnished truth—demanded their attention.

Dred poked at the wrinkled half-tomato sagging under bread crumbs, eyed the two pieces of steamed broccoli and the small spiral of puree. "How considerate. They don't want us to overeat."

Dahlia cut into her swordfish. "Where was I?"

"Rocking and rolling."

"Ah, that's right. In sync, in harmony. Then, all of a sudden, he reared up. His eyes rolled all the way back. His body shuddered. He groaned."

"Wow, that's what I call a climax!"

"Climax?" Dahlia shook her head. "He dropped dead."

"Smothered in love, what a way to go."

Dahlia hunched her shoulders, whispered. "That's what he did, Dred, *go*."

Mildred Trusdale stopped sopping up lemon butter. "You mean he pooped on you?"

"No, no, no. He died."

"Died!" The word shot out of Dred's mouth in a shout. Heads turned. Men stared. Dred mopped up spilled water with her napkin.

"Let me help you." Young and Handsome appeared with extra napkins, laid one on the wet tablecloth, shook out the other on Dred's lap. "There. No harm done." He sailed away into an ocean of suits.

"Dead as a doornail." Dahlia's hand shook as she lifted her glass.

"You were the death of him," Dred hissed.

"I was not!" Dahlia banged her fork against the plate.

"Okay, okay. Heaven blessed him with the climax of a lifetime. How did you explain that to the cops?"

"Well, by the time I wiggled out from under him my mind began to function again. I felt awful. The *poor* fellow." Dahlia chugged the last of her wine. "Finish up, Dred."

"You first."

"All I could think of was what was I going to say? I had a dead man in my room in a very compromising position." Dahlia looked at her old friend with beseeching eyes. "What sort of person would they think I was?"

Dred lowered her glass. "The kiss of death?"

Peals of laughter ricocheted around the room. Some suits swiveled around.

"Oh, Dred, you kill me!" Dahlia daintily dabbed her eyes. "But it wasn't funny back then. Oh, no. And I had a problem."

"Yep. A naked dead man in your bed."

"That wasn't the problem."

"That's not a problem?"

"I couldn't identify him."

"Yep, that's a problem. But you knew him."

"His body yes, his name no."

"Definitely a night to remember."

A server in white hovered at Dred's elbow. She swabbed up the last bit of sauce and nodded. Then he whisked away Dahlia's plate, the knife and fork, tines down, crossed atop the cold gray fillet. Dred's eyes followed the dead fish.

"It was dry," Dahlia sighed.

"Unlike carnal knowledge. Or a police report. Dahlia Livingston, recently arrived from the boring Midwest, admitted to having sexual relations with John Doe, address unknown. Through the actions of the known party with the unknown party, said unknown party died in known party's arms. Or, rather, in her. Period. A crime of passion in action. *In flagrante*."

"You always were good at Latin. Teacher's pet."

Dred pushed her glass away. "Then what?"

"I got dressed and...."

"Skipped town."

"No, Dred, that would have been irresponsible. I went to the bar."

"Would you care for something sweet now?" Young and Handsome looked from one to the other, his delicious smile hinted at exceptional delights.

"I'd love something rich and sinful," Dahlia purred through parted lips. "What would you suggest?"

Young and Handsome paused, "We have an exciting array of desserts and sweets."

"Control yourself, Dahlia. Think of the calories."

Dahlia pouted, her lips a bouquet of possibilities. "You're very tempting," she shot Young and Handsome a slow sidelong glance, "but Dred's right. I can't. Really, I can't." Dahlia drew a breath, "But I can have a brandy. Can you bring us both a glass?"

"My pleasure."

Dred dropped her voice, "You went cruising while a naked man got rigid and rock hard under the sheets?"

"Of course not, Dred! Though I could have used a drink. Speak of the devil."

Dahlia snatched the snifter as soon as the server put it down, wrapped both hands around the bell of the glass.

"So why back to the bar?"

"To find my friend, enlist his aid."

"What for, to dress the dead?"

A ripple of suits trickled toward the door.

"No, silly! He was a regular, not quite a barfly, but close. He probably knew the man in my bed. And there my friend was, glued to a stool. I pulled him outside, told him what happened."

"What did he say?"

"That lucky stiff." Dahlia's luscious tomato lips sagged into a sulk. "And, of course, he didn't know the man at all."

"So where to from there?"

"Inside, to order drinks."

"You bellied up to the bar? Drinking while Mr. No Name turned stone cold and board stiff?"

"It wasn't like that at all. My friend started chatting up the bartender. In a roundabout way he wheedled the poor man's name out of him."

Dred pulled the brandy glass closer. "Nice work by a nice guy to identify a stranger in the night."

Dahlia sucked the sweetness off her lips. "A perfect gentleman. He pledged to remain silent as the tomb about the whole affair. I promised to do the same and sealed it with a kiss.

"What a nightmare. The *police!* Well, Miss Livingston, how did it happen?" She rolled her dark eyes. "I nearly died of embarrassment."

"What did you say? Balling the jack?"

"Mildred Trusdale, that is absolutely beneath you! Really, Dred, I don't know what kind of people you run around with. The vulgarity!"

"Did the cops laugh?"

"No, they were perfect gentlemen, the one taking notes never looked up from his pad, not even when I said we were merely letting nature take its course." Dahlia hoisted the snifter to her lips. "Still, it was a sobering experience. I took off for Europe as soon as I could, swore off men, too."

"Yeah, who needs a track record as Killer Lips, the Grim Reaper's handmaiden in hip huggers." Dred tipped her glass, sipped the dark sweet liquid.

"Then one day it hit me." Dahlia threw up her hands, "*I* wasn't the dead one. *He* was." She smacked her lips in a brandy kiss. "So I got on with living."

The Old Man

He props open the door, the large lenses of his glasses glitter with sunlight falling off the neighbor's roof. Smaller than before, back now bent, he watches three people walk away. They connect him to the past, to his place in it. He stands, unmoving except to raise one hand. Crabbed fingers grab air. It is not a wave of goodbye but one of come back.

Just before the wrought iron gate, one of the three turns, waves and smiles at the slight figure caught behind a screen. Not much distance separates them, just a concrete walkway between now and before, long as a lifetime.

Love
and
War

MIRROR IMAGE

My Gram came to visit. I love it when she comes. My Daddy brings her. She used to drive her big car but she told Mommy she didn't like driving at night, so now Daddy picks her up and drives her home.

Gram brought me a beautiful doll this time. Dolly has thick brown curls and big blue eyes with lots of eyelashes. She brought Tommy a dump truck, but he doesn't like trucks. I told him to tell Gram he wants a helicopter instead. But he didn't. He thinks it's not nice to ask for something. He's silly. Big brothers should know better.

Daddy says Gram is old, that's why she doesn't like to drive at night. But I don't think she is. When Gram was waiting for Mommy to bring her coffee, I went close to her chair and said you're not old Gram. You're still beautiful. Gram hugged me tight and gave me lots of lipstick kisses. Tommy smiled at Gram, too, and she gave him a kiss and said you look just like your father. Tommy was happy to hear that, but I don't think Gram was happy to say it.

Today I saw a beautiful dress with lots of lace and a wide wide skirt. It was the color of a ripe peach. Soft and sweet. I asked Mommy to buy me the dress. She said no, I would get tired of it after wearing it once or twice. I promised I would wear it everyday. Mommy still shook her head. Too expensive. I told her Gram would buy it for me. Don't you dare ask. That's what Mommy said. She doesn't know me at all. I won't ask. I'll just tell Gram I saw the most beautiful dress in the whole wide world. Gram will buy it for me I know. Gram says I'm her little girl, I'm just like her.

Mother Love

For most, a chance at life comes but once. For me, the chance came in '35 when a soldier's uniform I first wore. Taught me to drive, the army did, back when few knew how and the only cars on the road belonged to the army and the police, the rich and the shrewd.

Mustered out, returned to the mill with a license to drive and the first overcoat I ever owned. Straight back to the Count's fields I went, sharecropping as of old. One day a stranger came to the mill where my family lived still, though the Great War had long ago forced us off the river and onto the land. Shattered the great millstone, those warring armies did. Then the waterwheel churned uselessly with the Viarsa's slow push.

When the stranger came to the mill, my mother stood at the open hearth stirring polenta in a copper pot. The key to the cupboard tied to her waist glinting with fire. My father stood at the door, shouted my name louder than the noon bells.

Offered me a job, that stranger. Driving one of his trucks delivering whatever needed delivering. Maybe a special trip, maybe days away, but always with special pay.

No sooner had the stranger crossed the courtyard did my mother speak, her voice shiny and sharp as metal. "What nonsense he talks."

"Steady work, steady pay. No matter the weather, no matter the season," I said, thinking I'd be free.

"The wheat won't wait. Nor the corn. Who will till the land? Your father is too old, your sister too weak, your brother too busy. Who but you can fill the cupboard?" Sidled up to me, her back already beginning to bow. "Who but you can take care of us, your old parents?"

Fourteen, I was, when first yoked to family and landowner. Only the army broke their hold, but just for two years. A man grown and not yet married, I was, when that stranger came. Listened to my mother, I did. Let my chance at life slip away. But a chance I had. Not so Delia.

My sister was the firstborn, I the last, separated by seven years. Delia had watched a brother die and another burn. The river spoke to her, as it did to my father, spoke of miracles lived and wonders seen in times when the world was small and the misery deep. No beauty, my sister, with her eyes of clear gray like river pools under too much sun. Long of face, cheekbones high, a crown of rich curling hair of harvest brown. Grace she had, wearing hand sewn clothes with the bearing of one born to better things, but the pigs, the garden and the kitchen were hers to tend.

For her, as for all, the time of loving arrived. For her, the suitor with a lock on her heart was a farmer strong of back and set of will. Guido was his name. When first I heard Guido's name I was not a boy but not yet a man.

"Guido, Guido asked me to pledge. He wants a sign of intent, of consent. I would say yes." Shivered with delight, Delia did.

Beneath her black shawl, long fringe caught in the folds of her black skirt, my mother counseled, "Too soon to promise. There is time for such things. Tell him not yet, not now. If he truly loves you, he will wait." Brushing a hand against her apron bared the key tied at her waist, the metal caught yellow lamplight, winked an evil glint. "Time, time you have."

Guido proved true. Yet, always he asked, always Delia answered, "Wait." And he waited. And his resolve hardened. Then, on an evening set aside for courting, Guido stood at the mill door. Delia stacked the last dish onto the worn table by the stone sink, readied herself for their time together.

Later, words I can still hear pierced the dark of the mill. "Guido, Guido will leave, work in another land, build a future. A new life he wants. Sure he is in this, he will wait no longer." Sobs stabbed Delia's words. "Choose to go, or choose to stay, but choose you must." Like a stalk of wheat broken by whirling wind, Delia bowed before my mother. Release, Delia wanted. A blessing.

"Just words. You will see. Guido won't go. A few Sundays, and he will be back at our door." Sharp and cold as ice, my mother's voice. "Wait, he will be back."

Sundays passed. How many I cannot say. Others sought my sister with her crown of curling hair and demeanor of a queen, but none reached her heart. Then word traveled the village to the mill. On a day marked by chance Delia saw Guido from afar. At his side, a woman from a nearby village. Man and wife boarded the train, took a chance at life.

Then time it was for me to leave. The army sent me to an unknown realm, and gave me a skill. Showed me things to astonish and confound as I drove men and papers all around the Deep South. One time, went to Foggia to deliver documents and stopped to see a friend stationed there, he came from a village not far from mine. Welcome it was for us to speak Friulano, recall places and customs we knew and wonder at the people and ways of doing in that strange land where shoeless men wore suits to sit idle while their women worked the fields. That day, a whim took me to the railroad depot. An unease held me there watching the trains coming and going. One bound for Bari waited at the platform. Windows sometimes dark, sometimes bright. Passengers sometimes dozing, sometimes awake. All waiting.

Only afterwards, back at the mill, did I learn Delia was on that very train to Bari. How long she stayed away I do not recall, heavy with work I was. Details of why she left birthplace and parents to be a housemaid for strangers never did I hear.

Delia returned to the mill to be what she was before: housemaid to my mother. With her she brought back a skill. Got to be known for her deft hand in the kitchen. Cooked many a wedding feast for others, but never one for herself. A life spent in shadow, Delia.

Seasoned, she was. The villagers whispered she carried the odor of something left too long. No suitors appeared at the mill door. Delia bore her fate with grace, kept to the old ways and reveled in the stories my father told of the river and of times past.

Long after my mother was gone, her words proved true. Returned, Guido did. His hair gray, his face written by work. He came to the mill where Delia lived still. Guido found her in the garden, bent beneath the blue of a September day. Together, they sat in the kitchen, the door open to air holding the promise of change. They spoke as they had never spoken before, of the years in between, of the family Guido raised, the wife he buried. They spoke of their youth, the dances under the stars, the dreams they held but never shared. And when the sun was low in the sky Guido stood on the threshold of the mill, bid Delia goodbye.

Told me of Guido's visit, Delia did. Told me long afterwards, her gray eyes shimmering. She lay in a hospital bed, asking to go home to the mill. Not yet, I lied, the doctors say to wait. Wait. Even now, thinking of my sister, alone and dying, the cancer gnawing her to a bone, I hear my mother's cold voice cutting sharp and deep. Hear her say that word, wait, twisting it like a key to lock Delia away from a chance at life.

Paulin di Romano

Good natured, Paulin. Such a welcome, Paulin's big laugh! Warm and hearty, like the loaves fresh from the bakery oven next door. Both laughter and aroma floated out to greet you with what was good each day. Ready and quick, Paulin, tending the wives flocking to his shop at midmorning. Kept the line moving, served each in order, though a few tried to cut ahead. He just smiled, kept to slicing mortadella, all the while listening to their chatter.

"Oh, oh such pain," one farmwife complained, lifting a leg marbled with bulging veins.

"Not as bad as mine," replied another with legs of a bull. A finger thick as a whip pointed, "Inside, so deep."

"And me? Did you know I was so sick I was already dead?" asked a third woman, so thin a rail would be put to shame.

"Are you throwing up yet?" Dorina patted Lina's tummy.

"For days now," Lina smiled proudly.

"Both due the same, are you?" Paulin's laugh big as his smile, knowing well what lay ahead for them. Him having watched his wife walk that path years before. Knew, he did, that each mother-to-be likes to think she's the first-mother-that-ever-was.

Most of those gossips knew Paulin's story, but it was stale. Fresher news rendered better results. Only thing to remind oldtimers about his story was what he wore: numbers and symbols tattooed blue on an arm. Souvenirs of the war. Marked him, the Russians did. So many POWs there were, they branded them like cattle.

Paulin had marched away wearing Mussolini's uniform, the feathered cap of the bersagliere. Wore and did what he was told to do, an inductee like most from villages like ours. Off to see a world they didn't know and didn't want. Il Duce dreamt conquest, garnered defeat and even worse, shame. Four years it took for the Allies to end the war.

All the while Paulin's father Romano kept his hope quiet. Even when word came Russians had captured his oldest son. Others in the village were captives of the Russians in the Great War. They returned, stepped back into their lives. Cobblers and tailors and farmers still, watching the same scene play out again. But home they came. So might Paulin.

Got so though the thought of Paulin grew into a knot of pain in Romano's neck. Worked, he did, to ease the ache, worked under the sun in the vineyard. His wife and daughter tended to the gaggle of gossips coming to the shop.

Was out in a field cutting hay with a scythe, cutting straw to bed the chickens he kept. Sky was fresh, swept clean by wind. A stranger came to the meadow's edge, called out, "Are you Romano, the father of Paulin who went to Russia?" Romano let the scythe drop to his side, the sharp point jabbing air. "I have news of Paulin," the stranger said. Romano stood still, feared what his ears might hear. "Paulin's alive. It'll be some time, but home he'll come." With a roar to heaven, Romano hurled the scythe into the sky, the blade slicing circles of blue.

Weeks and months slid together, still no Paulin. The family waited. Worry and doubt slipped in between hope and expectation.

Was a day so clear and bright it almost hurt to look at the green and yellow of the fields, the copper green bulbs topping the white church tower. Even the train overpass above the dip in the road to the village seemed scrubbed clean by light.

Out of the gray of that underpass came a man brisk of step dressed in the leftovers of a uniform. In one hand he carried a slack rucksack, the other swung free.

Alda dal Giornal spotted him, her newspaper shop being at the corner of the main street and the path to the cemetery. Alda squinted against the light, her jaw dropped.

The man turned, "Bon dì, Alda!"

"Sestu? Is it you," Alda exclaimed. "Paulin, Paulin di Romano, is that you?"

Paulin grinned, "Sigûr, soi iò. Tornât finalmenti! For sure, it's me. I'm back at last!" With a wave, Paulin walked straight ahead. Walked straight into his father Romano's shop.

Of course, you can imagine the hubbub. Word tore across village and field. Paulin, have you heard? Paulin is back. No! Can it be so? Paulin? Returned? The voice rode waves of light and air.

And like a miracle a demijohn of wine appeared on a chair in front of Romano's shop, glasses stacked for everyone to toast his son Paulin's return.

Oh, so crowded the store was those first days! There Paulin was, behind the counter just like before the army took him. Just like before, Paulin di Romano's hearty voice greeted you, warm as the sun.

Never lost its luster, his deep rich laugh. Never lost that branding in blue either. No, no matter how long, how hard that time in Russia, nothing killed the hope, the joy, all the things that made Paulin, Paulin.

BREAD AND BUTTER

The eldest son crossed the street, climbed a flight of stairs and walked through the swinging door. The cooks were sitting on overturned crates or on chairs around a large tabletop balanced on a square table, rice bowls in their hands. He faced them, repeated what his mother had instructed him to say. The cooks kept chewing. One of them, a fellow with gray hair and tired eyes, put his bowl on the table, laid his chopsticks on top of it. At the stove, wok shoved against a backboard splattered with grease, he picked up a giant pot, scraped the rice crust free. The browned kernels fell into the pail the boy handed to him. Old rice stuck to another pot fell in sticky slabs.

The boy carried the bucket across the busy street, his body tilted to one side. Through the deep doorway he stepped into the dark beauty parlor, then down a long hall. The telltale odor grew stronger the closer he got to the back room.

His mother stood at the stove, stirring a wide deep pot. She eyed the rice grounds in his bucket, dumped them into boiling mash. She was making whiskey, rice wine, the bread and butter for this fatherless family.

Dream House

The mother and her youngest daughter stood next to a small window. Outside light slid in, skimmed the edge of a work bench, skated across a smooth cement floor, skidded to the raised walk-in closet built of wood. The room was dry, clean, spacious. Their first basement.

The daughter counted three unpacked boxes in a corner, looked up at the rafters. Spaced along the middle beam, two bulbs wore metal hats and beaded chains. Next to the angled steps to the kitchen the owner had put a light above the handyman's table, a vise still screwed into the corner. He used it to build the storage space where the mother's old fur coat hung next to the new Persian lamb. The daughter corrected herself. Not the owner, the former owner. Her mother and Jimmy, her stepfather, owned the bungalow now. The mother's dream house.

The daughter smiled, "Nice."

The mother nodded, eyes bright, hands clasped to her chest. Light picked at her blunt fingers, worn and starting to warp.

A familiar beat of three raised the daughter's head towards the usual spot on the floor above. "I thought Jimmy went to work already."

"He did." The mother's eyes flickered. "Why do you say that?"

"The footsteps. I thought they were his."

"What footsteps?"

The outside light faltered, the inside air cooled.

"Didn't you hear? Sounds. Like someone's walking." The daughter shrugged away her mother's stare. "I've heard them before. Must be the house settling."

The mother's small body knotted. "Where, show me where you hear them."

They stood between kitchen and dining room, the daughter pointed to the floor where creaks had broken the quiet of being home alone, the after-school hours graying outside. The daughter answered questions of when, how often, how many. "Three steps, always three," she said, waving away uneasiness. "It's the house. It's settling, that's all."

The next time she sat at the blond dining table, she nudged the ring of the ceiling light suspended overhead. It gently rose, riding a cord wound on a small pulley. She smiled, nice. Spreading out books, she filled lined notebook paper with words inked in permanent blue. Behind her the window darkened between slats flattened into slits.

At the first footfall she fixed her eyes on the sound. Two more steps. She studied the spot where unseen feet paced. A chill made her shift in the straight chair. She looked up, saw an unexpected face.

No longer did the picture of Jimmy in his GI uniform smile at her. Instead, her father looked somewhere beyond her. His death portrait had hung above the dining table in Chinatown, then moved here to the unheated sewing room in the back. Now, once again he kept watch in the dining room.

A key grated in the front door. The mother, unspeaking, walked straight into the kitchen. Her unseeing gaze marked by three worry lines furrowed between wrinkled eyebrows forewarned the daughter. Tearing paper, clacking crockery announced the mother's return. She placed a platter of cooked chicken on the low cabinet beneath the father's picture, took out two short glasses from the cabinet. In one she poured a shot of whiskey, in the other she propped an incense stick. She dropped a sheaf of rough paper, some plain, some covered with thick brushstrokes into a metal wastepaper can. A match rasped, flames curled. Black Chinese characters charred into black flakes. The fire burned its shadow onto the inside of the red can bordered in white teardrops.

The daughter sat opposite the mother in the kitchen nook, the platter of chicken between them. Above, a halo of lamplight embraced them.

"It was Daddy." The mother rested her hand, the chopsticks slack between tired fingers. "His footsteps."

A grain of rice caught in the daughter's throat.

"He's not happy in the new house. I offered him food, drink. To content him." She looked at her lastborn with lusterless eyes. "I burned paper money, paper clothes, so he would go away. Wouldn't hurt you." The words dropped, slow as tears into her rice bowl.

The daughter pushed against what she heard behind the words. "It's the house, Ma. Just the house."

It took some time for the daughter to notice. The footsteps stopped.

CARL AND PEG

When Peg dyed her hair pink Carl figured they were in crisis. He dumped his wire rims for thick square frames and took to wearing all black. Peg took a look at his new look and pierced her right nostril where it crinkled. Carl didn't say a word but shuddered every time she reached for a tissue. An ear was easier, though the noise of the needle in his lobe sounded like Niagara Falls and nearly made him barf up breakfast. Peg took a look at the ear stud, faux gold, and sniffed. Carl cringed, closed his eyes as he listened to her blow.

Carl's mood matched his clothes. He and Peg were teetering on the brink, and Carl's vertigo kicked in on any brink. He walked to work it out. He veered toward South of Market. Nerd Nirvana. Hip Town.

A flyer was taped to a wrought iron gate.

> You're invited to a special event at the Cave: The opening of Dispissations, a new exhibit of recent works by acclaimed artist Bakar Bulubek. Come to not only see extraordinary art, but also to find out more about Cave classes and literary events. Friday, 6:00 to 8:00 PM. Refreshments will be served. FREE.

Free fit Carl's budget, and a walk down avant garde lane might be just the juice needed to jazz up a sagging relationship.

Friday night found Carl leading pink-headed, mini-flounced, bare-armed Peg down Bryant, dark with six story brick buildings and minimal street lighting. It was 6:15. One half of the iron gate was cracked open to allow entry to an alcove with two locked doors, one bright bulb and one elevator lined in recycled wood slats. Carl and Peg stepped out on the second floor. A sheet of instructions in bold red type tacked to a bulletin board read: The last person out shut off the lights, lock the door and set the alarm.

Carl carefully turned the silver knob to the blue steel door. The foyer was empty, a short hall led to a dark office. A large picture stared at them. The images were small, tightly packed without an inch of space to spare. Peg paused before the drawing, pink head dropped to one side looking for the artist's signature. Carl eyed an oversized penis draped over a stop sign.

A man in a long sleeve blue shirt holding a plastic cup sauntered over to another canvas of equal size and crowdedness. A woman's voice floated from a room. Blue Shirt followed it. Peg followed Blue Shirt. Carl followed Peg after he made out the name Bakar Bulubek among the squiggles drawn at bottom right.

A motley group of men, women and children of all ages and sizes formed a half-circle to face an odd arrangement to the left of the door. The structure looked like a picture frame, minus the picture, standing on end. Around the open frame opaque tubing ran along the top and down one side to the table where a mop of yellow hair with bedraggled brown tips was propped on a white column.

Peg touched her pink hair. The wig matched her true hair color, dingy blonde. She adjusted the broad straps of her loose top to look careless like the cherry tank top draped over tiger tights worn by an attendee with purple hair.

Carl spotted a table at the back littered with empty bottles and manhandled paper plates. He swallowed. They'd missed the refreshments.

The director of the Cave introduced Blue Shirt as Bakar Bulubek. "This event involves bodily fluids," the artist said, rolling up his right sleeve. Carl shifted his feet, which bodily fluids? Bakar's assistant, a guy approaching midlife who might have been the father of one of the prepubescent girls sitting on their heels at the front of the crowd brushed the blonde wig. The hair fanned out neatly into an even fringe around the plastic prop. The Assistant Dad turned to the onlookers. "My help is not necessarily an endorsement," he said to titters and smiles. Then he picked up a small plastic tray. Bakar grabbed a paper square, ripped it open, extracted a needle and stabbed it into the crook of his right elbow. Peg gasped. Carl gaped. Bakar then jabbed the end of the tube hanging on the pictureless frame onto the needle in his arm.

Peg flinched. Carl groaned. Nothing happened. Bakar muttered. The needle went from bent elbow to trash bin while the AD tore open another packet. This time Bakar hit a vein. Three loud thumps scared Carl's eyes back open. The tube was stiff with blood, the wig hopped up and landed with another round of loud thuds.

Blood began to course through Carl's arm. Peg left pink imprints as she let go. Bakar muttered again. Someone in the crowd shouted, "Try the other arm." Bakar rolled up his left sleeve, the Assistant Dad freed another needle.

Hand in hand, Carl and Peg hurried out the blue steel door. It quietly closed them out of the Cave.

Food Fight

"That crass remark was totally unwarranted." Dahlia fanned thick lashes over her big browns. "I merely said he was cute." She sniffed deep, tipped her chin up.

Dred read the signs, familiar since high school journalism class. "All I said was you never met a man you didn't like."

"Mine was a perfectly innocent comment about a perfectly behaved deliveryman doing his job. How can you jump to conclusions and make sweeping statements like that?" Dahlia slammed knives down onto the embroidered tablecloth. A pizza box held center, flaps tucked in husbanding heat. Wine glasses winked red in waning summer light.

"Stop stewing," Dred said, "let's eat."

Dahlia popped the lid, flattened cardboard to the table. "Has there ever been an occasion when you kept your mouth shut?"

Dred reached for a wedge fragrant with herbs and heavy with topping. "Since when did you develop a thin skin?" She nipped the sagging tip, tongued melted cheese into a cheek. "See, my mouth is shut," she said chewing.

"Well, that *is* a first worthy of applause." Dahlia eyed her best friend. "What if I said you never met a meal you didn't eat. How's that?" She stabbed a fork into her pizza slice, a knife held at the ready.

"Not true. There's that much vaunted andouille sausage you raved about in Paris that stank like armpit and tasted like toilet. I couldn't stomach it, as you may recall."

"That's right, go ahead and blame me for your poor palate."

Dred stopped chewing. "Cut the fat."

"Fat? What fat? This is pizza, though I would have preferred something less greasy than sausage. But that's what you wanted. A taste of home, as you put it."

"What's wrong with having Midwestern food in the heart of Heidi land? Spill it, Dahlia. What's your beef? My plebeian tastes?" Dred's tone was as level as her gaze.

"Let's not bicker over food."

"Come on, Dahlia, lay it on the table."

"Well, if you really insist, I take exception to your reference to my appreciation of men. You seem to think it's a fault." Dahlia's red lips crumpled like a smashed tomato.

"Look, the guy was delivering pizza, not Sir Galahad coming to carry you away from the humdrum. You ogled him like he was a hunk of prime rib."

"See, see! It's always food with you. Everything for the body, nothing for the soul. Nothing to sustain the sensibilities of beauty, physical or otherwise."

"Mostly otherwise in your case, Dahlia. Sex. Real or imagined. An undeniable appetite carnal to the core." Dred lifted another large slab of pizza, counted how many pieces were left.

"That's not true! I aspire to rise above, not to surrender to base instincts."

"Sure. That's why you skipped watching "The Kingdom of the Shades" so you and the guy sitting next to you could get to know each other better. After the two of you hit it off during intermission you decided a chat over confit de canard and Côtes du Rhône wine would result in a better performance than any ballet."

"How dare you paint such a tawdry picture of a perfectly spontaneous sharing of minds! Besides, it wasn't duck. We had a splendid meal of fresh shellfish artfully arranged on a three-tier silver server. And champagne. *And* he was a perfect gentleman."

"Nothing like feeding the soul at a five star restaurant. Cheers!" Dred hoisted her glass, guzzled. "See, you met a man and a meal you liked that time."

"Why must it always come down to men?"

"It's your favorite spice to add pizzazz to a life of boiled potatoes and crackers, the extent of your culinary skills." Dred muffled a belch. "Wasn't that why you appointed Jonathan as house chef? A good one, too. His beef burgundy really hit the spot."

"Don't bring him up. Jonathan was always a fool."

"Well, he did propose and you did say yes. And he was chief cook and bottle washer for, what, thirty years? Too bad you sent him packing."

"I did not send him packing! He chose to go."

"Chose, smoze. Say, wasn't it your foray into haute cuisine that finished it? Roast duck. Or was it smoked duck, so smoked the billows brought two screaming fire trucks?"

"Don't exaggerate, Dred. I merely forgot to turn down the oven. The duck fat—there is a lot of fat on duck, you should be very careful how much of it you eat, Dred—caught fire a teensy bit. I tried to explain that to the firemen, but *no*, Jonathan had to interrupt. Imagine, telling all those men I knew absolutely nothing about cooking! How humiliating."

"And that cooked his goose. Poor Jonathan." Dred noticed the congealed cheese on the last slice. "But it worked out in the long run. He got a chance to get a gander at a spring chicken, then bingo, he's adding joy juice to his steaks for her. And you got to dine in on homemade salad or order a la carte wherever beefcake waiters served. And, who knows, maybe a handsome man joined you for conversation, champagne and company."

"Honestly, Dred, what are you saying? Salad is slimming. You should try it, it might help."

"I'm saying you never met a man you didn't like. Actually, Mae West said that, and she said it to Cary Grant when he was young and she wasn't. Or was it, come up and see me sometime?"

"Must you persistently dwell on innuendo and double entendre. It's annoying, Dred."

"What, Dahlia, you don't like guys?"

"Of course I do. But in moderation. Which is not what you exercise when it comes to fat, the lard for arteries. Cholesterol is simply bad taste. And, it wreaks havoc on your waist."

"Fat is flavor. And look who's talking moderation, Miss Cholesterol on the Half-Shell. Besides, do you really think by chewing less fat I could give the slip to the Guy with the Scythe? Croaking is the way of life. The last supper. The end of the gravy train. I rather drop like an ox eating high on the hog than linger long on bland and boring." Dred paused, skewered Dahlia with a pointed look. "What about the last piece of pizza?"

"Oh, take it! Just don't croak at the table." Dahlia lifted her chin, "and Jonathan's beef bourguignon was far too salty."

Pool Ducks

The pair swam close together, he in the lead by a stroke, she at his side. They wove a slow pattern on the still surface. The apartments fronting the pool were quiet, like the timid light creeping over the rooftops. Silently, the two ducks took wing as one.

The old man watched the sleek iridescent green male lead his mate away. They disappeared to a place he could not reach. He settled deeper in the chair, his large eyes fixed on the calm blue pool beyond the window. Though his chest was layered in cotton and flannel shirts, sleeveless vest, red wool sweater over a gray one, his hands were cold. The cane the Medicare nurse brought him rested beside feet layered in socks.

"My legs are weak," he had complained when the nurse first helped him step from couch to sitting chair. "That's why you need to keep walking. Just two more steps each day. That's how you make your legs strong again." The exercises helped, but not as much as the leg massages his wife Mae gave him every morning and night.

The old man closed his eyes, rubbed them. They were dry. He blinked, trying to see. It had all come at once. The move from the familiar to the unfamiliar. His legs giving out. The trips to Emergency. How did he who once was in control come to this, sitting in a chair and looking out the window? Fumbling, he found the eye drops, one ran down his smooth cheek quick as a tear.

He thought he saw a reflection on the water. He stood, shuffled to the window, hoped the birds from heaven had come once more. The water riffled with the breath of a breeze. The old man felt chill, stepped back. Then, slipping out of the pale light into the shimmering blue, the pair swam together again, one beside the other, silent and serene. The old man smiled, at peace.

TUG OF WAR

Seven, there were. The Great War was over, armistice signed some two Novembers earlier. But the seven from Friuli, like many from other nations, languished in a camp. No one knew how to get the prisoners back home. Siberia was far, wide as the sky, bleak as war. Russia was in revolution, more dangerous to cross than in war. So soldiers squatted on the gray land, troops housed by nation, each represented by a legate of their own.

A gray spring arose, moved toward summer. Legations got together, decided to leaven confinement with competition, games between groups. The seven from our village, including a pair of brothers, formed a team. The Italian legate came to see them before the match. By then villages like ours below the Julian Alps no longer belonged to Austria and the seven from Friuli had become Italian citizens with a stroke of a pen. That legate made a promise, a promise sweet to hear. Vowed he would do all he could to bring the seven home if they beat the French in a tug of war.

Even, the match was. French and Friulani equal in strength and endurance. Each team strained to pull the other across a gray line scratched into the gray ground. The rope taut with pride and prowess. The Friulano leader, Jacum by name, sensed his men tiring. Shouted in Friulano, the language of their birth. "Hold steady! Don't waste energy. Let the French tug and pull. When they weaken, we act.

"Now do like me," Jacum commanded, working his heel into the ground. "Dig!" He hollowed out a pocket in the dirt, planted his heel in the hole and braced himself, taut rope in hand. Each of his men heeled a hole and anchored a foot to ease the strain.

Twenty minutes it took. Twenty minutes of holding firm. Then Jacum saw the French wince with pain from palms sawed raw, eyes weary in sweaty faces. "Now!" Jacum shouted, and the Friulani heaved as one, dragged the French across the dusty line.

Kept his word, that Italian legate. Took some doing, but managed. Sent the seven born in a village of dirt roads and poor schooling on a journey none could ever have imagined. Sent them to the Golden Horn. Reached Vladivostok by foot, cart and train. Crossroads, Vladivostok, China and Russia coming together at the Sea of Japan. Waited some more, those seven. Even had time enough to sit for a formal portrait.

Then set off on a seafaring ship, the first they had ever seen. Long it took to cross a vast sea, endless as the barren vastness of Russia, to reach the bright vastness of the New World. San Francisco, a jumble of languages and people, hills and water. Boarded a train there, a train that traveled days to cross a continent of mountains, plains, prairies, hills, hamlets and cities all the way to New York.

Set sail once again, crossed an older ocean. Landed where Christopher Columbus was born. From Genoa the train carried them closer to what they knew. Finally, they stepped back into village life as farmers, tailors, cobblers. One cobbler, Jacum's younger brother Valentìn, dug his future out of a pile of manure. More than one witnessed Valentìn shoveling, then unwrapping and cleaning the sewing machine he'd oiled and buried, hiding it where no advancing army would look while he was away at war.

And that picture taken in Vladivostok bore witness. Each of the seven uniformed in brimmed hat and tight leggings. Four seated in front, legs crossed at the knee. Three standing behind, left hand on hip. Centered between men sitting on his right and left, a boy shorter on his feet than the men in their chairs. Hair cut close, eyes frightened, a basket of flowers in his hands, feet shod in cloth shoes. Chinese he was. Most likely alone and far from home. Jacum, seated in the front row. A small smile lifted his mustache, touched his eyes. Pleased he was, knowing he and his team were going home because they dug in their heels.

What's in a Name

Must have been 1943, maybe '44. Not long after Nazis took over. SS came to the village, made us farmers line up in the piazza. Scared, we were. For what, and why did they collect us like chickens in a cage? Stood there in our work clothes, blue jackets and pants, bare feet or wearing zoccoli of wood caked in mud, heads covered more often than not by a soft cap, blue too. Those birilli saved us from the sun's rays but left our eyes free to see.

Let us know who was in charge, the SS did. Ordered us to take those caps off, wanted to see our faces good. Stood there, who knows how long. Us sharecroppers getting drunk with sun and dizzy with fear. Let us go. All of us. Even Checo Piron.

Left the village, those Germans. Straight. Correct. Roared away in their cars and trucks thundering under the train overpass. Nazis took a set of rails early on. Needed the steel, needed it to make tanks to fight the Allies. Trains coming and going forced to share a single track, kept the stationmaster busy manning the switches.

No surprise it should have been. Them coming back. Nazis came looking for a certain Francesco Sedon, sometimes called Checo, Checo Sedon. But no Sedon there was among us. A villager, who knows who or why, sent the Germans to Checo Piron instead. Loaded him into an armored car, put him in prison in Guriza.

Not someone you notice, Checo Piron. A quiet sort, not given to big gestures or bold moves. No quicker or slower in wit than most. A good son. A ready worker. And what did this Francesco Sedon—the man Checo Piron was supposed to be—do to make the Nazis want him? Checo Piron never knew, Germans never said.

Tried, his parents did, to get Checo back. Got one who worked at the castle, Nazi headquarters by then, to ask the aide to the German general to get Checo released. Decent, the aide was. A man caught in war like the rest of us. Tried, the aide did, but nothing to do.

Then a worker at the railyard at Guriza sent word to Checo's family. Checo was bound for Germany. Weeping, his mother wrapped bread and cheese in a cloth, packed a change of clothes in a rucksack. Sent her younger son Toni to the train station. Crouched low on the family bicycle, he raced toward the depot. At a checkpoint Toni had to show his pass. Reached the station just in time. Toni spotted Checo in the third to last wagon. Hugged each other, each crying, the packets from home handed from brother to brother. The train whistled, left the station.

Stopped in Udin. Longtime crossroads, Udin. Longobards, Attila, barbarians of all sorts passed through heading south for better things. Checo stood at the chained railcar door looking long at what he knew. Then, on the next track, a train headed toward the village shuddered to a stop. A wagon door faced Checo. Behind it stood a man he knew. Startled, both were. Where are you going the villager asked. Germany, Checo said.

Quick, the villager looked around. Checked the passageway behind him. Spoke softly so only Checo could hear. Listen, nobody's here. Jump over. No one will see. In the village, we can hide you. Come!

The engine stoked up. Checo shivered. Wheels creaked. The villager threw open his door, waved for Checo to jump. But it was too late.

Blew up the locomotive, the partigiani did. Resistance fighters dynamited the tracks at a tight passage between a steep village hugging rock and a dense forest sloping down deep. Escaped, many did. But not Checo.

May of '45, war ended. Before it did, villagers witnessed things never dreamed. Germans, stalwart, strong, handsome, disappeared overnight. Ruthless Chetniks, partisans they called themselves, took over City Hall, then vanished into the woods. Days thick with Allied bombers. Blotted out the sun, so many there were. Ranks of stiff-armed soldiers in turbans marched with the British. Americans driving boxes like cars set up headquarters in the castle. The war walked right through the village.

But still no news of Checo. Us sharecroppers worked the land, followed the seasons, gave half of what we grew to the landowners just as always, war or no war.

Then word came. Survivors of the German camps were coming home. Toni and his parents went to the same station in Udin where Checo was last seen. Walked the long train looking for Checo. Didn't see him. Fear got to twisting their insides. Then a voice called out, familiar it was, but not the face. Crying, they embraced Checo, carried him home.

Twenty-seven kilos. The weight of a good-sized child, that's what Checo weighed. Months, who knows how many, Checo stayed in the sanitarium, getting back to who he was. But never did he work the fields again. Couldn't. Dachau—what he saw, what he did at that concentration camp—seized his hand. Turned it inward. Couldn't uncurl his fingers, Checo, no matter how hard he tried. Stayed that way, not open or closed, long as I can remember.

Payment Due

"Hallo!" Dieter approached the man stationed behind the bar, shelves of bottles behind him. "English, you speak English, don't you? Everyone speaks English nowadays."

Thanos prided himself on being a Greek who served the island men first, yet took care to welcome the occasional vacationer with the same hospitality he gave his own. He eyed the tourist, his hair so blond it seemed white, his sure step, confident bearing. His grating voice raked away the afternoon quiet. Thanos ignored the irritation tingling below the surface. He wiped a damp cloth across dark wood, cleaned everything away. "Yes, I speak English. Italian. German. Some French. But English is best."

"I used to know some Greek, years ago. Now, no more." Dieter turned to the entryway, nodded to a rawboned woman with fair hair and a teen blond like his father blinking sunlight away in sudden shadow.

"I used to come here a lot, oh, maybe twenty-five years ago." Dieter's laugh warmed cool blue eyes with memories. "The taverna remains as I remember it!"

"Twenty-five years ago? That was…."

Dieter waved a hand, a wide ring of worked silver caught light. "Yes, yes, the war. A bad time. But it's over!" Dieter glanced at his wife walking toward a small table. His son roamed the room, looking at trays of moussaka, pastitsio, lamb and chicken displayed behind glass. "Forgotten."

"You know the island from the war?" Thanos allowed himself to remember.

"We're here on vacation. Beautiful! So beautiful. The same. I was afraid the island would be changed like so much has. All for the better. Good times. Prosperity. Those days, fighting, fighting everywhere, everyone. Different now. But not this taverna, still the same."

"Years pass, but they make no difference to the sea, the hills. This island of men. This place."

"Sure, I told Monika, my wife, we came here after being on patrol, maybe in the rain, and here, here it was always warm. We got a drink, maybe ouzo, maybe retsina, what was on hand." Dieter beckoned his wife. "Let's have some ouzo." Dieter slapped a hand against the countertop, fingers spread like barren branches.

At the sound Thanos glanced at the man's hand, saw a ring of wrought silver against dark wood. He twisted around to the wall of bottles. His gaze lingered on a small frame of olive wood propped in a corner. The face of a young man with dark hair swept to one side and eyes dancing with mischief looked back at him. Thanos grabbed a clear bottle, took two small glasses, poured. "What about him? He looks old enough."

Dieter smiled wide, eyes on his son. "He's 16."

"Old enough." Thanos poured a third glass. "Some fighters in the war were that age. Times don't change that much."

"Yes, yes, you're right. Gunter, come here." Dieter waved away his wife's protests. "Watch alcohol turn to milk!"

Thanos tipped a small carafe. Water turned the colorless ouzo cloudy. The family's laughter was bright and loud. Thanos watched them. The woman must have been a beauty before motherhood took hold, like his own Marika had been. Now cosmetics kept her young. But Marika wore what life granted her. She was at his side when his father made him swear.

"Come, pour me another and one for yourself. For old times." Pale color seeped into Dieter's tight cheeks. "I came back here, put things into place."

The tall bottle hovered over Dieter's glass, another glass stood ready on the bar. Thanos eyed the German. "Tell me when you were here last. Was it the winter of '43-'44?"

"Terrible time. Rain everyday, and cold. Patrols day and night. Ambushes." Clear ouzo turned murky. "It wasn't always like that on the island, but that year, towards the end...."

"Yes, it was a time of war." Thanos looked down. "Lives lost."

Dieter nodded, his pale blue eyes seeing snatches of the past. "We were lucky. We survived." He snapped to the present. "We had a 25th reunion. The men in my unit came from all over Germany to celebrate. Celebrate being alive. Some brought tokens, souvenirs, from those times.

"Souvenirs?"

"Oh, small things, a talisman, something from a dear one." Dieter cast a sidewise glance at Monika. "A reminder of home. The things that got us through the war."

"Such as the silver ring you wear?" Thanos captured Dieter's blue eyes in a steady gaze.

"This ring?" Surprise lifted Dieter's voice. "This ring comes from Athens, a trinket I got on leave."

"The design is unusual."

"It's one of a kind, that's why I purchased it."

"My father saw such a ring once. He described it to me often after that night."

"That night?" Dieter's blue eyes clouded.

"It was as you said. Rain swept the hill, rushed to the beach and out to sea. Winter cold and early darkness had slowed the fighting. But that night, the night my father first saw a ring like yours, was different. Men from the island took their hunting rifles and firearms brought back from faraway places, climbed to the hilltop woods above this taverna. Four partisans laid in wait for the Nazi patrol. Three came back. What happened to the fourth none of the three knew."

"Why...what are you saying?" Dieter riveted pale eyes on the barman's face, peeled away years and flesh to find the young man within.

"The fourth was found at dawn. He was in a cleft of the hill. His leg and side were bloodied, his hands tied, a bullet in his head." Monika and Gunter froze, watched from a table.

Dieter struggled against the memory, released a hoarse whisper. "The war."

"The war." Thanos bent low, reached down beneath the counter. "My father never would have known about that night, known how his son and my brother was captured, executed, except for the boasts of a Nazi soldier drunk on ouzo. A young man who wore a silver ring. I swore to my father that I would never forget."

Dieter staggered. The sound of the bullet blasted away time, filled a moment. A woman screamed, a chair slammed against cement.

Thanos laid the gun on the bar. He turned to the smiling face in the picture, raised his glass in salute.

First Encounter

A stranger's face. Sandpaper cloth on skin. Her twisting away to escape, squirming legs pinned tighter. Her arms reaching, screaming tears, ballooning snot.

Daddy sat at the head of the table, Eddie next to him, the girls along the arms. Ma stood at the kitchen door. They were all smiling, laughing. Nobody would help her.

The memory wove in and out, threaded through years. Snatches appeared in dreams, flashed with feelings. With time she stitched shreds of scenes into a patchwork of the past.

That rough army fabric marked their meeting. He had tossed his duffel bag out of a troop train, jumped off with his officer's okay as it rolled past Chinatown. He came home from World War II just in time for dinner. He picked her up, the sister born while he was overseas, and held her tight. The firstborn and the last child together for the first time.

KEPT SECRET

George Kozick of Chicago stood back, watched long rollers sweep to shore. Six hundred feet out, gulls skimmed swells where the underwater undulations began. He knew how deep those camouflaged troughs were. He squinted against incessant light. The sea looked as he had never seen it.

The rising sensation was familiar, that nighttime cramping. Sweat glazed his forehead. Fingers of wind ruffled white hair, thick and coarse as an old military brush. He blocked sunlight from his eyes, ordered his mind to stanch rolls of nausea. Once again he felt the rough thrust of the sea, the gut wrenching plunge, heard staccato bursts, random shrieks.

"Sir, sir, are you all right?" The light voice lifted with a French lilt.

George Kozick sensed the tour guide before he felt her hand on his clammy arm. He opened eyes blue as his mother's and stared into a face fringed in fine dark hair. She must be Linda's age. His favorite granddaughter was a mother now, like this woman might be. What was the guide's name? Karin, that was it.

"Yes." The lie stalled in George's throat. He shifted his gaze toward the headlands lying to the right. Three beaches lay beyond. Wind, persistent and timeless, pushed waves aslant as it had that day. So much pushing.

"Sir, are you sure you are well? Is there pain? You cry."

George ratcheted air, rammed down the midnight onslaught. "Pain?" He nodded, "I need, I need to speak."

Karin tilted her head in sharp light, watched a proud crown of white bow. With her body she shielded him against wind and curious sunbathers. She left him space enough to breathe.

"Tell somebody." His voice sank as his strength ebbed like water swallowed by sand.

"Yes, I am here. I can listen." Karin scanned the picture takers, the row of beach bungalows not yet shaded by the steep cliff behind, her van parked among tour buses. She stepped closer, held him in her eyes. Once, he might have been too tall for her but now burdened by years he was within reach. "There is time."

"No, not anymore." George parsed his words between gasps.

Karin, patient as with a child newly walking, waited.

George Kozick looked beyond the Frenchwoman, young as this day, to where a terse blue line slashed across a sky flushed white. The distant sea, calm. Deceptive.

"I was," he halted. The past careened into the present. Nightmare images converged, bombarded senses. George fought to speak, "...a tank commander."

That day came back whole. He had stood staring at the long stretch of dingy brown wracked by a leaden sea dark with threat and cloud. A broad bluff, thick with green, stood guard. A rush of boats sped into heaving swells of gunmetal gray. From them men surged into the churning sea, disappeared, dragged under by heavy packs.

Survivors struggled ashore, unarmed, unprotected. Soldiers huddled among hedgehogs, giant crossed iron rods encased in concrete lying at the shoreline like jumping jacks of child's play, demon toys to tear into the heart

of ships and men. Starbursts, smoke, spewed from the
guardian cliff. Artillery played across the beach, pocked
the water. Still the men came, came in waves like the
unforgiving sea.

The first tanks rolling off the amphibious transports
sank. Too far from shore. George Kozich felt the landing
craft slow beneath him, heard the squad leader shouting
move closer, the pilot yelling can't, won't be able to get
off the beach. The squad leader cocked his pistol, pointed
it at the pilot saying move closer or I'll blow your brains
out. George Kozick's stomach lurched, his tank rattled off
the ramp, dropped. Spray stung his eyes, salted his lips.

Karin stood still as death next to the commander of
old, fighting for air.

"We gained traction." George Kozick spotted a ma-
levolent flash amid mottled green. He shouted the coor-
dinates, the cannon obeyed. But something caught his
attention.

"The sea, the water was alive."

The woman whose father counted but a year of life
on that day sixty years ago held deep her breath, fixed
her kind eyes on the white haired soldier who was not a
warrior.

"Bodies. All around. Arms reaching. Fingers clawing.
Legs running." The old man's neat blue shirt, cinched
tight at a still trim waist, shuddered with the telling. His
feet, shod in sturdy black shoes polished as his youth had
been, sank deep into sodden sand. "The wounded, the
dead, bobbing like toys."

A breeze brushed Karin's hair, dark as a sparrow's
wing in flight.

George Kozick of Chicago raised his eyes, screaming in his ears. Gulls swooped above his head. But what he saw was the beach of that day pawed by relentless waves. And that straggling line of khaki stretched too far across a beach too wide.

"I tried to maneuver, find a way around the bodies." Each word ripped a hole in long kept silence. "There were so many. We had to cover the guys on the beach. Fight."

Karin placed her hand on his shaking arm, her touch as light as his young granddaughter's head resting on his chest had been.

"Forward, I commanded."

The wind slipped between the old man and the young woman, carried blinding nightmare images, tank treads sucking and grinding, comrades fallen in battle, helpless in death mangled by metal. The cry of a gull floated overhead, a long roller curled beneath itself, swept back to sea. Unchecked tears flushed out an old wound.

"Sir, it was what you had to do." Karin's voice was low and calm. "It was the war."

"Omaha Beach," whispered George Kozick of Chicago, laying his dead to rest.

Name Game

Born of the same mother and of the same father, the three brothers bore the same surname. Yet, they went to their graves with no common name. Mussolini forced them to choose. For the glory of the new Rome, Il Duce decreed those under his rule must bear surnames that sounded of Roman legions marching into history, not of invaders or barbarians or men born on the land long before there was a Rome. Henchmen loyal to Il Duce tramped into the old farmstead with their big boots and bigger voices. Menace steeled Mussolini's men, weighted their words proclaiming Il Duce's latest decree.

The brothers Carnich, a name rooted in the ravaged earth of Friuli, had farmed their father's land under his watchful eye. But now, men full grown with children of their own, bitter discord over their father's patrimony turned brother against brother. Refused outright to share a surname. Each lived by his own creed and cunning, so each considered, then chose.

The oldest, Marino, Nino to fellow fieldsmen, walked to the village, kicked the soil off his wooden zoccoli and entered City Hall. Told the clerk that he decided on Carni in place of Carnich. Some say the Carni, a fierce and proud tribe, fought the first Romans long and hard. Lost, they did, and their blood seeped away like rainwater washing over Roman stones, but their name is woven into that of Carnia, a stubborn mountainous corner of old Friuli. Reborn, Nino was, as Carni, Marino.

The second Carnich son stood less ready to go the way of Rome, yet sought a smooth path. He entered City Hall as Sigismondo Carnich and walked out as Sigismondo Carnicco. Neither Roman nor Friulano he was. A change in spelling and sound to mimic the names of those in power. A middling name for the middle son.

But the third, the youngest Carnich, held fast, like his ancestors had in the face of disaster and onslaught. Enrico Carnich he was born and Enrico Carnich he would remain. No surprise it was Rico, as he was known, clung to birthright and heritage. No surprise either Rico was belittled and bullied by believers in Mussolini. Forced, Rico was, to drink a bottle of castor oil. Fascists laughed and pointed as Rico walked tight-legged, struggling not to soil himself on the way home. Often summoned to City Hall to pay fines for infractions of laws known only to fascists, Rico withstood all, paying the price for the name Carnich.

The Allies roared into the village, GIs took over the castle overlooking the fields of the brothers. Like gentle rain soaking parched soil, benessere came to Friuli. The good life even reached our village of hills and vines nestled between mountain and sea.

The brothers prospered, each in his own way. Nino's son, a Carni, studied to be a doctor, left the farm of his father far behind. Sigismondo Carnicco's son became a grocer, opened a shop in Guriza. But Rico Carnich's son remained true to the land, a winegrower of some fame he is. Friuli, long overlooked, has come to earn a name for its wine, once grown and drunk only by Friulani, now shared with the world. Some say Rico's face, lined like this land of rivers and runnels, and his vineyard, now tended by his son, were pictured in a foreign magazine in America, but this I have not seen.

La Stuchera

Me and Zaneto Bocal got called up in '35. Me to Potenza, him to Abruzzo. The longest and furthest we'd ever been from home. Twenty, we were. Zaneto, not a big man, liked acting like one. Got so his voice grew to be the man he thought himself to be, especially after Spain.

Some things stick, a seed in your teeth. Some things stay, a first of something good. Or something bad. Some things grow old with you. That's the way with La Stuchera. Not much to speak of, La Stuchera, a stone bridge jumping a runnel you can't see but can smell when the heat's high and the wind's down. Nothing much leads to La Stuchera and nothing much runs from that little bridge. Just there, part of everyday. No recollection why the name. Mention La Stuchera though, and everyone knows where you mean. Cross it fast as a sneeze by car now. Still the best way to Cormons.

Evenings, me and Zaneto Bocal used to bicycle across La Stuchera, icy as a spinster's heart or singing with mosquitoes. We rode to Cormons to dance with the policeman's eight good looking daughters. Their mother sat on a raised chair to keep an eye on who was touching who.

Me and Zaneto mustered out after two years. For me, it was back to sharecropping for the Count. Zaneto, now, took up Mussolini's offer, volunteered for Spain. Came back loaded with money, bought a nice house. Family lives there still.

Picked up new ways of doing things, Zaneto. Messy time, those days before the war, but not as bad as at the end. Zaneto kept to what he'd learned, kept to bullying in the tavern and out. Then him and me got called up again, the war closer. Him to the militia in Cormons. Me to a village in the Yugoslav hills. But those in Rome got to thinking maybe I might side with the Slavs, so sent me home. Zaneto, instead, felt right inside his uniform.

Loved to sing, Zaneto. Nice deep voice. The loudest of the fascists in song. Toadies told us to gather wherever they wanted farmers on display. Zaneto handed out fake shovels of cardboard, work clothes of loose threads or pressed paper mended with glue, all to be paid for out of our sharecropper earnings. Threatened and manhandled complainers, Zaneto, all the while braying about military might, the glory of Rome. To me, no good ever came out of Rome.

Worked nights, Zaneto did, and nights I had free. Cut through fields, a thicket of chestnuts and oaks to reach a friend's place over the next ridge when I rounded a bend.

Flames where they shouldn't be, voices rough and loud pounding hard against walls. Enough twilight to fix on a white farmhouse, catch red tongues licking at insides. A mattress tossed from a window hit the ground, split, scattered stuffing of corn leaves.

A voice I knew in song and in curse rose as night fell. A family, clinging to each other, crying. Slovene farmers. Lived on the land for generations like us, spoke like us, worked like us under the same uncaring sun for uncaring landowners. Now, by decree, deemed outsiders. Zaneto, sure in his might, sure in his right, used his big voice. Get out! No Slavs here! Only Italians!

Turned into the darkness, all I could do. A stranger, he was, this Zaneto born in the place of the companion I knew in youth, the one jumping deep into the pool of the old quarry to pull Edi up to air and light. The Zaneto who bicycled with me over La Stuchera to eye the young ladies.

La Stuchera. A bridge so slight it seemed a trickster's tease sidling beside the raised railroad bed, the hill to a red castle ahead. A few pedals more brought you to a dirt path cut straight to the heart of the castle. Once, maybe twice, a year fancy carriages pulled by fancy horses would bring people in all sorts of finery to the Count's fancy ball. The castle lit by oil lamps and candles, the electricity Mussolini promised being too weak to get beyond the piazza. Maybe a car or two among the horses prancing between rows of cypresses furled like umbrellas. Stood stiff like soldiers, those trees. Then a whirlwind snapped them to pieces long after the whirlwind that made La Stuchera stick in my mind.

The war arrived. Blackshirts in the village. They left. The Germans took over the castle. The Allies landed in Italy. The Nazis left in the night. Chetniks occupied City Hall, left for the forests. Chetniks, Tito's partisans, and Italian partigiani fought Nazis and each other. They all faded into the hills. No matter to Zaneto, true to his uniform.

Like leaves rustling in a breeze, whispers spread from village to farm, across field and hill, touched every house and ear. The Allies were coming. Villagers dared to hope, change was coming. They rallied in the piazza. Hard and fast, Zaneto bullied into the crowd. Dodging Zaneto's militia car, men swore, fisted the air.

Late, the spring of '45. Frost slow to give ground, brown slow to grow green. But that morning woke clear and clean. A voice, big and full, sang awake birds. No reason not to sing. Zaneto, duty done, pedaled toward his big house, his young family. Zaneto's song announced his coming. Rising light picked out the handlebars, bright as a beacon. The castle on the hill watched, like it had watched the Nazis arrive and the Jewish count flee.

La Stuchera. A single crack sent chattering birds circling high. A single wheel circled still air, the other churned dead grass. Zaneto Bocal lay silent at the end of the little bridge.

Leftovers

Bianca carried a crimped paper bag, brown against her cheery yellow cardigan. Buttoned down to beige slacks, the sweater covered a pale yellow blouse with a precisely pressed collar. At a tight curve in the road she paused to catch her breath, rested a hand on a gray fence. A loose ring of gold caught a flicker of light sneaking between green leaves.

A silver SUV inched along the blacktop, wary of what lay beyond the bend. A sliver of color caught on gray wood rounded into view. The driver took note of the woman's pale hair and pale face, rolled down the window. "Are you okay? Can I give you a lift?"

"Oh, I'm fine, just taking my time." Bianca lifted full lips into a shadow of the smile that had won a GI's heart.

The driver heard wear and tear in the frayed words, leaned a scruffy head of too much hair out the window. "Sure? It's a pretty steep climb from here." Then added, "It's no bother," thinking of his grandmother's formality, her reluctance to relinquish independence.

"No, no, I'm fine. Thank you for stopping."

The driver moved forward past the slim brightness against gray and green, disappeared into the next curve.

Bianca smiled to herself. He must have been close to Vic's age when he roared into the village with all the other Americans. So long ago. When they were young, swept up with what was changing the world, remaking it as none could ever imagine. Now they were old. Left over. Like the risotto ai frutti di mare she carried home for tonight's dinner.

At one time, not so long ago, she would have disdained taking home leftovers. Not so long ago, she would have prepared her own risotto in her own home. Tended it with care, adding shrimp, scallops, calamari, fish and ladles of homemade broth to arborio rice. A risotto her own mother had never made. Who could afford such abundance back when hardship was easy to find but meat was hard to put on the table? Italy, at war. America was different. Everything was possible. Change was constant.

Unimaginable changes. Even in Italy. Young people— her own niece, the daughter of her dead brother—lived openly with a man as if married. Nobody in the village blinked an eye. Divorce, commonplace. Rules discarded, none put in their place. The world moved faster than she or her GI could. They had been left behind, he in a nursing home, she in their daughter's basement.

Bianca crested the next rise, paused under trees to breathe deep. Her daughter was right. It had opened her eyes to go beyond this winding road, walk into town, try the local restaurant known for its authentic Italian cuisine. She would tell her daughter when she came home from work. Tell her the food was closer to authentic than the swill she had first tasted long ago in this land of immigrants. But it wasn't authentic.

Below her she saw her daughter's home buried in trees, cut off except for a narrow road leading to a lost village.

Chance
and
Destiny

ROAD WORK

Winston Klahr signaled and pulled over, watched tits jiggle and hips hike out of mirror range before rolling down the window. Blowzy blonde holding it together with peasant blouse and ankle skirt, brown eyes unnaturally bright. All purpose backpack that's been around too long and to nowhere good. His blue eyes tightened behind black wraparound shades. "Where are you headed?"

"Anywhere along the Embarcadero."

"I'm going to the Financial District. I can drop you off at a choice spot."

"Great!"

Winston checked the rear view mirror for police as she tucked her skirt inside, slid the backpack between her legs. Feet needed washing, flipflops crusted in brown.

"Gee, I've never ridden in a Jaguar before." She smiled into his sunglasses, dropped her eyes to the dashboard, let them wander over the wood trim. "It's nice."

Winston heard the honey in her voice.

"You're nice to pick me up."

He noticed her voice dropped a notch and her boudoir smile. As expected. He knew what was running through her mind. "All in a day's work."

"What kind of work do you?"

"Cut a little here, slash a bit there. You know."

"Oh, a number cruncher. I should have figured—Financial District."

"What are you?" Winston knew, but he wanted to hear her say it.

"Me? I'm an artist." She washed her palms together.

"That's what I thought. From your look."

"Living, being at one with nature is an art, you know." She tilted her chin to give him a sidewise smile.

Unadulterated sunlight pointed out what she had taken pains to hide. The scar under her left ear was neat, clean, sharp. "A nature lover and artist. What else do you do?"

"Read human nature."

"Really?" Winston veered onto the exit ramp. He waited to hear what he wanted.

"Where are we going?"

He heard surprise, then wariness. He stifled a smile. "Short cut. Bottleneck ahead." Trees whipped by, huddled closer in steep twists.

"This isn't the way I know." She lifted the lumpy backpack onto her lap.

"Don't worry. I know this road." He glanced into the rear view mirror. No cars. None ahead.

"I don't want you to go out of your way." Red flecked fingers played with pocket flaps.

"No worries." Winston sped up. "You'll get to where you're going. Trust me." He slowed at a deep dip, trees cut them from view on all sides. He turned to her profile, followed her sleeve. He expected her hand to fumble at the door handle, the one he'd locked with the child-proof control button. Her hand flicked fast into canvas folds. His smirk died.

"Now," she said, "this is a nice secluded spot." She looked at him with bedroom eyes that lied, lips that curled.

He should have known. He stopped.

"Get out," she said sweetly. The silver snub nose gun in her hand never wavered.

La Primuda

Once upon a time in the middle of the last century when my grandfather's father was young, long before the Great War plowed up the mountains and mowed down a generation, back when the land and the river were the only means of living for all but a very few, a sharecropper was hurrying along. As fast as you can hurry when you're riding on a cart drawn by two oxen. Ox may be bigger and stronger but they're no faster than cows. Was spring, the season of drenching downpours and cherries of every red. Young roses of every color, vines surging into full leaf. None of that means a thing, though, when you've got a task to do and you're trying to beat the sun climbing in the sky.

Farmer's snapping a whip above the oxen's heads. They're plodding along in the mud left by a temperamental rain cloud, paying him little mind, heads sawing sideways, tails beating the air. Suddenly, an ox stops, then the other lurches to a standstill, the wagon wheels sink into the mud. The whip's darting over the oxen like a dragonfly dodging the names the farmer's hurling onto their bowed heads. Thunderstruck, and blind, that's what the animals seem to be. One ox collapses to its knees. Then the other kneels in the mud. No matter how loud the sharecropper shouts and flicks his whip, he can't get them to budge.

Down he climbs from the cart, muttering curses thick as the muck sucking at his bare feet. He makes his way in front of the kneeling animals and is about to let loose with the kind of language that makes a priest quail in his cassock when he notices their eyes. Looking right past him, like he's not there. Not only that, there's a peculiar glow in their eyes. Unnatural.

The oxen stare steadfastly at a tangle of brush. The sharecropper sees something caught in the glistening leaves. He slogs through the sticky mire and beats back branches. Then the stiffening dissolves in his legs, his knees buckle.

Don't ask me how, but clothed in fresh green, wearing a halo of wild roses woven into a pink crown, stands the Madonna, untouched by rain or mud. Serene. Why and how did that statue get there? No priest would leave it in the woods. No farmer or landowner would lug the Virgin Mary with him on his rounds, no matter how pious he might be. And no one would plant Mary in a bush for safekeeping. If she fell off a wagon or slipped out of a travel bundle, she'd be dirtied or damaged. So how? Maybe the oxen knew, but they couldn't say. No one could explain it away except for one thing: divine intervention. That's what the villagers said. A miracle, plain and simple.

Took a little while, as these things do, for the villagers to build a home for her, but that they did. To this day the statue of the Madonna that appeared to the oxen rests in a simple chapel. That humble shrine takes its name from the hill that holds it: La Primuda.

Conversations with Ghosts

Photos fluttered onto nubby wool flecked with beige. I stared at my hands, I was losing my grip. Kneeling, I gathered generations and decades, carefully closed fingers around faces and forms.

"What's the matter, Daughter?"

For a moment, both voice and question carried me back to Chinatown. On a summer night I had tired of playing by myself at the big table. Down the dim hallway to the darkened beauty parlor I walked to my mother's side. She sat on a peeling blue chair behind long lacquered slats tilted to the street so she could see people and cars on Conway Avenue.

I leaned against the hard roundness of my mother's knee, a sure island in the warm darkness. She asked what's the matter Daughter, and I answered I've got nothing to do. The sounds of traffic, summer bugs buzzing, and the tick of her thumbnail picking against the other filled the space between us. Then her voice came slow and low, you're lonely, Daughter. Only afterwards, a long time afterwards, did I understand her meaning.

Now, looking up I saw her small frame dusted in shadow. Beyond her, sunlight splintered through textured curtains. "The photographs just slipped through my fingers. I thought I was holding tight, Ma."

My mother smiled dimples into her cheeks. "I know, Daughter." She held the *o* in a slow caress that smoothed away years just as it once had soothed away fears of the only child left in a family of six. "At the old house, eight plates slipped right out of my hands. All I could do was walk around that broken pile. My grip was gone, Daughter."

"Old age catching up with me I guess." I sorted black and whites snapshots from color ones.

"Don't worry, Daughter. You got time."

"Come to keep me company, Ma, while I go through the pictures?"

"Big job, Daughter. Easy to lose track, get lost. Sometimes better to forget."

"Some are of people and places you know and I don't." I held a snapshot of a white woman sitting on a step of a white porch of a white clapboard house, my mother sat below her, legs outstretched. Both were young with bobbed black hair. "Who's this?"

"My friend Virginia. In Terre Haute. She taught me how to sew." My mother's dark eyes sparkled bright as the light of an August afternoon. "I made the outfits Number One and Number Two sons wore for a picture I sent back to China. Billy's was light blue and Eddie's a pale orange, the color of sweet melon.

"Photographer going from house to house, caught up with him at Virginia's, asked him to come to ours. Picture cost a dollar twenty-five. A lot of money those days. The Depression.

"Daddy's first wife had no sons, that's why he married me. I did my duty, two boys in a row. I couldn't believe my luck when Eddie was born. Wanted to pay respect to Number One Wife in China, sent that picture of both boys so she could see that Daddy's name would live."

Laughter, light as a breeze, made my mother a girl again. A photo escaped my stiff fingers, floated face up onto the floor.

Eddie's glare captured my mother and me, froze us in the time his rage beaded in black eyes cornered between bloated cheeks and crimped eyebrows. A bolt of stiff hair lunged over a frowning forehead. Pajamas buttoned tight strained against a trunk-thick throat shadowed by hanging chin skin.

My mother moved, silent as sun filtering through still leaves. The breath of her blue robe brushed across cream colored carpeting, hovered above her secondborn son.

"Eddie. Told Foster Mother about my life when she came to visit. No matter how we try, we can't make a go of it, I said. Is it my luck? She listened, looked at Eddie sitting in my lap. It is not your luck she said, it is your husband's. Eddie was like his father."

"It isn't fair. Daddy died at 48."

"Eddie was just like the other kids. Never played mean. Loyal. One time, boys ganged up on Billy. Eddie saw them, ran out to shoo them away, protect his big brother. The park swing started things going wrong."

My mother's words slowed, took us back to the other times we were home alone together, the rooms were different, the decades were different, but the end to her story was never different.

"Eddie fell off a swing, hit his head hard, bruised it bad."

Set free, the plank seat flew high, twisted on heavy steel links, then pitched downward, pointed corner first.

"Swing slammed right into the same spot where he just hit his head. I heard it hit. He was nine."

Eddie, rising from the ground, collided with blind and deaf fate.

"It took a long long time for the sore to heal."

The blow imprisoned Eddie at age nine.

"They tested his hearing at school. A social worker came, told me about a boarding school in Indiana. Teach him sign language. I did like she said, sent Eddie away.

"Each week, I gave two kids bus fare to visit him. Two hours going, two hours coming, two hours with him. I wanted to keep Eddie in the family."

"You did the best you could, Ma." I stretched to reach the picture, but Eddie slipped from my imperfect grip.

Eddie had always been outside my reach. His life was lived where he worked unloading vegetable crates, eating with his workmates, smoking cigarettes in the sun. Out the beauty parlor door with the break of day and back with dusk, Eddie slept in the room furthest from where I played house under the big table. I fancied him the bogeyman, clutched my dolly when I heard the beauty shop door slam against falling day. Footsteps and the squeak of springs, his only voice, told me he was in bed. I returned to my play, safe under an oilcloth roof and the watchful eye of my father. Below Daddy's death portrait a slim shelf held an offering, a glass of sand with an incense stick curled into a question mark of brown ash.

"I wanted Eddie to come live with us on South Street. Billy tried to convince him, told him he'd show him what bus to take. Get him to Chinatown on time for work. But Eddie said no. I left him behind."

"I remember, Ma."

Every two weeks my oldest brother ferried bags of laundry from a Chinatown apartment to a white kitchen. There, my mother examined, mended, washed and ironed all she had of Eddie. She stuffed tattered shopping bags with clean, neatly folded underwear, plaid work shirts, and dark corduroy pants. On top of one bulging bag balanced a carton of Camels, Eddie's pleasure.

"I wanted us to have Thanksgiving dinner together, a family. Asked Billy to ask him for me. Eddie said no."

Silence carried my mother and me to long ago Chinatown. A crushed block of light warped by a half-closed door divided where we lived from where my mother fixed hair. My mother had stood at the last bedroom, the one next to the shop.

"Eddie," she shouted through the caul of silence encasing her second son. "Tomorrow is Thanksgiving. We're having turkey. Come home for dinner."

From the end of the dark hallway I listened to bedsprings squeak.

"Sit at the table with the family, like before."

Bedsprings screeched. I crept to the room my big brothers shared, glimpsed Eddie's flailing right arm.

My mother stood, wordless. Again she called out his name. Again, Eddie shooed her away.

Stippled sunlight scattered shadows, patterned a small figure in blue. The robe hem rested by Eddie's fallen picture.

"He got sick."

"It's not your fault, Ma."

Tuberculosis thrived within Eddie's lean frame. They sent him to a state hospital. My mother visited him every week. I came home from my first year away, she took me with her.

Eddie knew his baby sister, hugged and kissed away the years.

Each week I rode the bus to where bungalows gave way to walled compounds. Kitty corner from the bus stop a gate opened onto a cemetery, the gate opposite opened onto the sanitarium.

Imprisoned within lime green walls, Eddie paced down wide hallways pocked with doors and broken by radiators to the tall window overlooking the front gate. The window was locked.

Each week I handed Eddie the nickels and dimes my mother wrapped with misshapen fingers into misshapen rolls of brown paper. They disappeared into the pocket of Eddie's robe, then the coins disappeared into the mouths of vending machines.

The summer stretched out, his robe stretched tighter and tighter, his glower grew blacker and blacker. As August straggled into September, I searched the lime green hallway, then found Eddie outside beneath the window looking out to the gate.

"Eddie," I shouted, smiled at his glance. "How are you?"

He turned away, faced the gate. The belt of his robe barely circled his waist. Sleeve cuffs crumpled against stitched pockets.

"Here, from Ma."

Eddie snatched brown fingers of papered coins from my palm with a nod. He directed his gaze to a place I couldn't see. We stood together, our separate worlds side by side.

"Eddie, Eddie, I wanted to let you know." I moved closer. "I'm going away, going back to college."

He shifted his gaze to mine.

"I can't come see you next week."

His eyes slid away.

"I'm sorry, Eddie." His sleeve was rough under my hand. I squeezed the solidness that was Eddie underneath. "I have to go."

For a time I stood there next to Eddie under an indifferent sky. Eddie shrugged his shoulders, nodded once, quick and short.

"Goodbye, Eddie."

I saw the wide black straps on my sandals against white gravel. I stopped, lifted my head, turned around. Through a stinging sheen of tears I searched for a figure clothed in pale colors that faded into a fragile orange, the shade of sweet melon. I raised my arm and waved wide, sobbing. Eddie freed a hand from a pocket, waved twice. "It's not fair," I heard myself say as I left him behind.

A breeze knocking against the window screen brought me back. Shifting clouds changed the texture of falling light, blurred lines.

My fingers plucked Eddie's photo from the floor, shuffled it among others. A wayward corner caught on a small square of color, knocked it free.

"Look!" I twisted around, held it high. "Remember, Ma?"

My mother sighed at the sight.

"The last time we saw Eddie."

It was November, dark skeleton trees lined the road. It was my first trip home from my home an ocean away. My sister drove, my mother kept her silence in the back seat, ticking one thumbnail against the other. It was our first visit to the new place where Eddie lived, a long time since any of us had seen him, even my mother because of what had happened at the sanitarium.

"He socked me," she said when I called from college. "Just turned around, hit me. Nurse made me bend over. So much blood. Dripped between my fingers."

All along Billy had kept nagging until it finally happened. Eddie got transferred to a modern facility in the center of the state, a nice facility the social workers assured my mother when they called. The picture I now held told the truth.

"Nice, wasn't it, Ma, to see Eddie? Look how trim he is, like I remember him in Chinatown."

My mother's dark eyes blurred, like they were in the picture. "He called out Ma when he saw me." Sadness tugged at her smile. "The first time since he was little."

"Look how happy he is." Lips pressed so tight into a grin it crinkled his eyes. "And the stuff he's holding on his lap. We brought shopping bags of gifts, remember?"

The picture quivered in my hand. The social workers had us pose, sat Eddie in a chair bracketed by his sisters smiling like fools. Somber, my mother took her place behind him, slowly placed one hand, then the other on Eddie's shoulders, reclaimed her son.

"It's unfair."

"What, Daughter?"

"For all that Eddie lived, why couldn't one of us have been there to hold his hand and say goodbye?"

"Your life is made before you, Daughter."

THE MUSKETEERS

Walter nicknamed them the Three Musketeers. The three hatchlings, cute fuzzballs, did what chicks do: peep, peck, poop and grow. They were Walter's physics experiment that proved a bust, nothing out of the ordinary happened to eggs bombarded with radiation.

Fate in the form of the Graduate Project Coordinator stepped in, announced that Walter had been granted a slot at an out-of-state physics forum. The GPC eyed the Musketeers in their radiated lab cage. "Now what are you going to do with the chicks, Walter?" What *was* Walter going to do about the Three Musketeers?

Dante adopted the Musketeers and brought them to a second story porch, put the chicks in a big box next to the mop and pail stored under the roof overhang. He named the trio Angela, Ajax and Hector and fed them scraps scrounged from friends eating at the Student Union. Ajax took to picking on Hector out of sheer jealousy. The teen rooster caught a slap whenever Dante saw him pecking Hector. Ajax would pause, consider the slap for five seconds, then bully Hector all over again.

As nights got longer and warmer, Ajax and Hector harkened to nature's call and crowed at all the wrong hours of the night. A neighbor lodged a noise complaint with the city. A fellow grad student took it upon himself to go to Dante's defense. Solomon, dressed in black, implied he was a county rep and reprimanded the neighbor for harassing Dante. The neighbor knocked at Dante's door, apologized, said he served in Italy during WWII. Seeing his neighbor, Dante felt bad for putting him in this position. After all, his neighbor had a right to a peaceful night's sleep.

So Dante loaded up Ajax, Hector and Angela in the back seat of his Ford Fairlane and drove to the experimental farms run by the university. He offered the trio to the poultry program.

The white-coated foreman flapped his arms, "No, no, no! Your chickens may be diseased!"

"There's nothing wrong with my chickens," Dante shouted back. "Your chickens are the ones full of disease!"

Luckily, Walter returned, volunteered to be deliveryman. He and Dante loaded Ajax and Hector, the two noisemakers, into the back of Walter's two-tone Buick. Walter drove a hundred thirty miles to deliver the roosters to his father, who promptly silenced them for stew.

Angela became the belle of the ball. She wore a long red string for Dante to hold on outings together. She sat in the bicycle basket on trips to the Student Union where she met Dante's friends and loaded up on leftovers. On the way home Angela worked off calories by waddling alongside the bicycle, the front wheel sweeping slowly from side to side.

On a memorable evening when Albinoni's oboe concerto played on a record player, a circle of six sat on the floor, and a pot of spaghetti boiled on the stove. Angela, escorted by Dante, made a grand entrance to the soiree. She nibbled at a single long strand of spaghetti, clucked, then mingled with the guests before heading home to roost.

Winter was nigh. Angela moved indoors. She poked around the garage with clucks and pecks, then returned to

Dante for a chuck under the chin and a scratch of her head. Dante left the ceiling light switched on for heat, built her a square nest of bricks covered by a grill padded with straw. In the bottom of the brick square Dante planted a light bulb to warm Angela's makeshift throne, provided a plank stairway for her to climb from floor to nest.

Everyday Dante visited her before classes and afterwards, bringing a doggie bag of goodies from Angela's fans at the Student Union. She put on weight. Her thighs thickened into formidable drumsticks. It took Angela more time and more effort to negotiate the gangplank to greet Dante and enjoy a tickle of feathers and nip a tasty tidbit. Always, in thanks, she ducked her head and clucked with pleasure.

The days grew warmer and longer. Angela perched at Dante's shoulder as they drove to the country. Rustum, a poli sci grad student, lived in the middle of farmland. Dante set Angela down on a patch of rich black soil. She clucked, squatted. A breeze ruffled red feathers. She clucked again, crouched lower. "She's out of her comfort zone." Dante picked up Angela, handed her to Rustum, a Student Union friend familiar with Angela's ways.

"She'll be okay here." Rustum planted her atop the porch railing.

Dante surveyed the greening fields. "Nothing's out there, is there? Dogs? A fox or something?"

Rustum shrugged. "Don't worry."

Each day before going to campus, Rustum perched Angela on the railing. She would be in the same spot when he returned. He carried her inside to roost. She laid an egg every other day. He stacked precarious piles of eggs against the fridge walls, squeamish about eating Angela's offspring.

One day Rustum came home later than usual. The railing was empty. Angela was nowhere in sight. A few red feathers lay on the ground. Rustum called Dante. Dante called Walter. "Angela's gone. We think a fox got her."

There was a long pause. Walter finally sighed, "Well, that's the end of the experiment."

BEAT THE DEVIL

That day, one man was not among us. That day back in '43 when the Nazis roared in, claimed the mayor's office. Collected us men like cattle from field and farmhouse. No escaping, though the voice had raced from villager to farmer. Couldn't outrun those German trucks, that voice running with fear. Methodical, the soldiers were. So it was a wonder when word later came about Pepe Tonut.

Lived on the edge of the village, Pepe did. In the Borc dal Diau. Off by itself, the Devil's Place, a rash of crowded houses, home to the poorest families.

A sharecropper Pepe was, one of many. Like every other landsmen in looks, but still looked like no one else. To hear his wife talk, Pepe was dirtier than most. His clothes collected mud like bees collect honey, and his ways of doing were sins against cleanliness. Had a reputation, Pepe's wife. No one, but no one, could call Rosella a sloven. Proud, she was, to keep everything neat and clean. Everything except Pepe.

Fact is, whenever Rosella washed the wood planks of the kitchen she refused Pepe entry at noontime. Didn't want him dirtying her fresh scrubbed floor. Made him sit on the cart in the courtyard. Brought him his minestra out there. Some women, the ones with wagging chins, said Rosella's hand with the spoon did not match her skill with the broom, her soup being more fit for shed than for kitchen.

So like spilled milk, word had spread to the Borc dal Diau that day. Soldiers herding men into the piazza.

Wasn't going to let anyone take Pepe. No, not Rosella. Quick, she called Pepe from the barn, helped him load an empty barrel onto the cart. Told Pepe to climb inside that barrel meant for grapes.

Rosella hitched the cow to the wagon, led it to a path skirting the piazza, headed straight for the vineyard. Nazis stopped her, asked where she was going. Looked them dead in the eye, her mouth grim like a scythe ready to strike. Said grapes needed tending and she was doing the job her husband wasn't doing, not with him standing there in the piazza. Believed her, those soldiers.

So Pepe and the cart rumbled onto the path gouged into the hillside. Passed trees hugging the dark slope overlooking terraces of vines growing under sun. Hid in those woods, Pepe. Rosella, now, gathered grapes, filled the barrel. Led cow and loaded cart back to the Borc dal Diau. After the Germans roared away and darkness claimed the hills, Pepe made his way home, safe and free.

Have to say it. Did what few could, Pepe and Rosella— beat the Nazis.

Lascia o Raddoppia?

Put Pordenone on the map, Paola Bolognani did. Young, blonde, buxom. Caused quite an uproar, almost a scandal, what she did back then when television was new.

Government owned the one TV station. Broadcast news. Or soccer games. Major teams. Few public programs, nothing big until *Lascia o Raddoppia?* with Mike Bongiorno. Caught attention, that quiz show. Barkeeps figured they could draw more customers by tuning in to *Lascia o Raddoppia?* on their TVs, sets being still too expensive for regular families to buy. Even women started going to bars to watch. Two or three sat at a table, mouths hanging open like a broken gate, watching and waiting. Their glass of gingerino untouched. Nobody, but nobody, was seen outside on a Thursday night. Death could stalk the village swinging his scythe and not a soul would he find to cut down.

Brought the show from America, Mike Bongiorno did. Questions put together by experts on all kinds of topics, and all kinds of amateur experts got quizzed each week on subjects like art, history, maybe geography. If the contestant made it through the first rounds of questions, he got put inside a booth tighter than a coffin. Had to wear a receiver on each ear to hear Mike. Nothing in that closed box except a telephone to talk and a clock to watch. Answered right, they won money, government money. Doesn't seem like much in today's lira, but back then those hundreds of thousands of liras were a fortune. Answer wrong, they lost a chance at more. Then, then, those who answered everything right week after week got the chance to take their winnings or double them—lascia o raddoppia. Answer right, win millions of liras. Answer wrong, lose it all and go home with nothing but disappointment in their pocket.

One woman, classical music her specialty, got that chance. She cried, poor woman, inside that booth. She knew she knew her music, but her mother was sick, needed the money. Sobbing, the woman gave up the chance for more, for glory, for fame. Because of her mamma. And all the women watching in the bars cried along with her. Life was up there on the television screen, real people with real chances. Real choices.

Mike Bongiorno had his own share of chance at the hands of fate. His mamma brought him from New York, where he was born, to her hometown of Turin when he was little. Divorced, Mike's mother and father, you could do that in America even way back then. Grew up in Italy, Mike did. When war came he left his studies, joined the partigiani, the Resistance. Him knowing English, the partigiani had him courier messages to the Allies. Had to sneak through woods, over a high pass to reach the Swiss underground. He got caught. Shoved against a wall, ready for shooting. Gestapo searched him, found hidden documents. American documents. Worth more alive than dead, Nazis figured. Sent him to prison in Milan, then on to a German concentration camp. Thought his luck had run out, Mike did. But chance stepped in, a swap of prisoners. Got shipped back to his father in New York. There, started living life again. Then took the chance that maybe, maybe, he could hit it big in Italy. Came here and hosted *Lascia o Raddoppia?* for RAI television.

Mike finally picked a topic each man in Italy felt he was a star—soccer. Way it went was Mike asked contestants to file out. Most walked out in suit and tie. But this time, the fourth contestant walked out in a skirt billowing from a tight waist and wearing high heels. You can imagine the hubbub in the bars, her like a fox prancing into a chicken coop. Shouts, jeers, gasps. All because of the unimaginable, a woman, walked onto the stage to do battle with men in the field of soccer.

Mike knew what was happening in bars across Italy, and went ahead like always. Asked her hometown, her job. So Paola Bolognani named a town in the middle of nowhere, a town in the flatlands of Friuli. She named Pordenone. And she was a student. More hubbub, an underage female on national television!

There she was for all to see. Blonde like Marilyn Monroe, body like Marilyn Monroe, and younger than Marilyn Monroe. Imagine! But she, too, had a mother who needed help. She, too, had only the hope of a chance to finance a future. *Lascia o Raddoppia?* was her chance.

Paola Bolognani stood in that booth and answered questions about the scores and winners from earlier years, even back to the '40s and '30s. Answered questions sometimes even before Mike finished asking them. What a wonder!

Got to be famous, Paola Bolognani, maybe even more popular than Mike Bongiorno. Women in the osteria laughed, maybe raised their glass of chinotto to challenge their husbands standing by the bar, heads shaking in disbelief, downing tajuts of wine to boost their manhood. Imagine, if you can, a woman of those times beating a man at his own game, at any game. Broke the mold, the Lioness of Pordenone.

No matter there was no father in her home to tutor her in the ways of soccer. No matter she had to learn what every man was born knowing. Paola Bolognani got a chance. And she took that chance, lascia o raddoppia. And won. Took the grand prize with her, walked away in her high heels and flouncy skirt. Pordenone even got promoted to provincial capital afterwards.

And Mike Bongiorno gave her that chance. Him knowing what chance and fate can do. Opened a whole new world, Mike Bongiorno.

It's The Life

On the ninth day, the bleeding stopped. The doctors didn't know why blood flowed from his insides. They'd tracked the flow to his stomach, but still couldn't stem the red stream. It stopped the way it started. On its own. Even so, they wouldn't let the old man leave the hospital. He hated that extra day in bed. The food was awful. He wanted to get home to his own cooking.

The doctors tried to explain away the unexplainable. Too many years of swallowing aspirin for his heart and taking too many pills for his gout. His stomach couldn't handle it. The old man let them talk, but he knew why he bled for nine days. His body was eliminating evil spirits, flushing out bad luck, cleansing away ill will, lies, slurs heaped on him. Now, with his body purged, he could go on anew.

THE GREEN

Horace Milton watched the street. He liked Kozy Korner. Not so much for the food and fair price or big portions but because of the window. A broad glass plate clear of curtains and clean of lettering. He liked watching the coming and going. Groups or pairs. Teens. Loners. Young marrieds. A mixed couple passed. He carried a child in his arms, she pushed a high tech stroller with more wheels and bumpers than any company car he ever drove.

That was after the war. The war. Funny how that time kept popping up these days, like the ads on his PC. PC. Personal Computer. Politically Correct. The jargon of the young who kept getting younger and called PC-speak communication. Line time on the phone or on the Net. Nothing face to face except the annual duty visit. His grandson kept yammering for him to upgrade, to get up to speed.

Getting up to speed. The amphibian had lumbered forward, slow, sickening. The swells subsided once the landing craft got past the atoll. He could hear his heart drumming in his ears. All the guys watching the white sand, the clumpy center of green getting closer.

They charged out, rifles ready, slogged through low tide and sucking sand. Milt, that's what the guys called him, glad to feel something solid under him, scared of the green. They hit the smooth lip, sand shifting under heavy boots. Then the point man, Logan, pitched forward, spreading red. Milt staggered past him, heard a splash behind. Kovac, somewhere in the sea. Milt crouched onto the beach, elbow-crawled. Sand scoured his skin. He lobbed toward lightning.

"How about more coffee?" Milt flinched. Wanda, holding a steaming glass carafe with an orange lip, noticed. "You okay?" She was his favorite server, friendly and efficient. Usually he heard the squeak of her waitress shoes coming up from behind. Usually.

"Sure, sure." He nudged the white cup with a smooth hand, pushed away six decades. He still didn't understand. Why him? When the cup was full enough, he sliced the air with a short swift handstroke. He sipped, savoring the warmth. His wife used to chide him, no wonder you have bad dreams, too much coffee. But her eyes told him she knew why he woke up sweating. She knew, but didn't know. Couldn't know.

The patrol had moved into the green, dense leaves that stuck, stunk of strange odors. Nothing like the green of snow country. Nothing singing. Nothing moving. Nothing they could see. Sweat clung to his skin, too thick to roll. The men moved deeper, closing in. Bayonet sharp rocks crunched underfoot. The green, like the enemy, waited.

Shots came from behind. Milt opened fire at where the sound last was while Mason pawed at the fallen man's chest. Nothing. They moved forward. Bunched up, hunched down, hunting. Two more volleys. Milt tore the green with a barrage of bullets. Silence. Milt went looking, found his buddy Trevor facing sky, his eyes wide and wet. Milt closed them. They moved closer to the center, more men fell.

Three of them left. Nerves tight. Eyes wide. Ears sharp. The green waited. Gunfire. Milt wheeled around. Buster on his knees, bleeding down to a trickle. They neared an opening in the green. Mason fired, then Milt. A bullet nicked a jagged rock at Milt's right. Mason dropped.

Milt, alone. He inhaled, steadied his hand. Cleared his head. He didn't have to look, he knew. No ammo. He gripped his rifle, stepped outside the green into the open. Stared across at shivering leaves.

A scrawny soldier, a Jap, rose from the green. His face glistened, his uniform streaked, his rifle pointed. Each moved forward. Could he do it, Milt wondered. Bayonet?

A crackle startled him. Wanda put the paper bag with his leftovers on the table. "You're awful jumpy today. Maybe you need some dessert. Apple pie is fresh made." She stood there in her platform tie-ups, her red hair piled high, red like her lipstick.

"Why," Milt mumbled. "Why?"

"What's that?"

"Nothing. Nothing." Milt smoothed the table with hands that were soft, unlined, unlike the inside of him. "Check, please."

He watched the window, noticed the afternoon light picking up details, making things clear, clearer than the sun at noon did.

He saw his young self facing another young soldier. Each, the last man standing. Alone, together. The green all around. Milt saw something familiar flicker in the dark eyes latched onto his.

Coins clinked onto the tabletop. Wanda swept away the coffee cup. Milt rose, slow and deliberate, looked out the window. Why him out of them all?

Milt saw that young soldier's face again, eyes glittering, mouth twisted. Saw him raise his rifle. Saw him throw it down hard. Wheel around, walk into the green.

"Don't forget." Wanda held up the paper bag.

"No, I won't forget." Milt pushed the door open, paused beneath a blue sky alive with light, then joined the others walking down a wide open street.

FIREBIRD

"I'm done on this side, turn me over." I read the quote twice. I didn't know how to take the words or the girl who had said them that fateful winter day. On December 1, 1958, eighty-seven students and three nuns died in the Our Lady of Angels school fire. Five more OLA students would die in the hospital.

In the fall of 1959 the high school freshman class assembled in the corridor: boys in single file, girls in a line. I heard talking. The shrill voice, somewhere between fingernails-on-a-blackboard and a buzz saw, caught the attention of a nun standing with feet apart, arms akimbo, mouth grim. *NO talking!*

The talker was a head taller than the two girls standing between us. Her stiff as straw hair, bleached to a failed blonde, curled an inch above the collar of her uniform blouse. She turned. The pallor of her profile, the ropy roughness of her cheek beneath colorless eyelashes made me remember my manners. I dropped my eyes, and saw her legs.

I gaped at a latticework of quarter-size scabs. The spacing between dead red wounds was even, regular, as if sewn by machine. The unbloodied skin was shiny, irregular in color, odd in texture.

Afterwards, the religion teacher asked the OLA students to stand. Nine girls and three boys got up. The blonde with the shrill voice and bad legs was the last to rise. Her name was Michele.

Until junior year I knew Michele only by reputation: funny, quick wit, tart tongue. That year I walked into the

Nest, the home of the student rag, and found Michele, legs stretched straight out, ankles crossed, hands in prayer position. Slowly, she separated her palms. Viscous opaque strings stretched, thinned, then snapped back against a palm. Michele clapped her hands coated with rubber cement again, unglued them once more.

Later, in a citywide student journalism contest, Michele won top honors with a concise essay comparing high school cliques to copies produced with clicks of a camera.

Later, I confessed that the first sight of her latticed legs had prompted an internal shout: Doesn't that girl ever wash her legs? Michele tossed back her thatch of blonde and roared.

Later, I learned Michele was burned over sixty percent of her body, her back on fire when she jumped from a second floor window. Seven good girlfriends died, the last at the hospital. Michele returned home after four-and-a-half months of surgeries and skin grafts.

Later, at a memorial service, a priest said the good die young. Michele wondered why she was still alive.

Later, I learned the bad skin on her cheek was a keloid scar, sure to signal the onset of winter by turning purple, and the bandages around her knees held together skin grafts torn open by the cold. I learned her lips were not naturally shaped like a pair of horizontal parentheses but fashioned by fire.

Later, Michele wanted to go to a dude ranch in Michigan and asked me to go along. She rode, I hung on to the saddle horn. Another summer, we dressed up and dined in a downtown restaurant. I finished off a lobster dinner with a dessert the waiter lit with a match. I didn't think he'd use kerosene I said, throwing up in the john. Fresh air worked wonders and I stepped into a shop, came out with a small white bag, offered her a piece. Michele stared for a second, you're eating chocolate marshmallow candy after getting sick? She dubbed me Garbage Guts.

Later, after a long hunt for a job that required no standing, Michele found one as a switchboard operator at a food company. One irate consumer complained of finding green lunch meat in a loaf of sliced bread. After disconnecting, Michele snapped, I should have told her she owed an extra sixty-five cents for the meat.

Later, Michele spent settlement money from the archdiocese on a house for her parents, a car for herself, and a cruise to Europe to kiss the Blarney Stone.

Later, Michele wrote a book about that fateful December day, *The Fire That Will Not Die*. In television interviews she appeared cool, self-possessed. And un-scarred.

Later, she sent a publicity picture. Michele wore a wide brimmed straw hat only she could carry off and a V-neck polka dot dress of white on black. With slim fingers gracefully bent under her chin, tarantula eyelashes, and lipstick-outlined mouth, she flirted with the camera.

Later, she established the Phoenix Institute dedicated to helping burn victims use and apply cosmetics to camouflage the ravages of fire. Self-confidence, self-worth was what it was all about.

Later, the fame would fade, the foundation founder, the pain flower.

Later, that fateful December day caught up with Michele, put her in a wheelchair, erased the vestiges of makeup and make believe, then released her on Independence Day, 2001.

Before that final fateful day, Michele had written:

> *I hope when I die people will remember the style I developed in life. I hope they remember how much fun we had and the troubled times we shared, and I hope I am not completely forgotten. I hope I have not developed to be this crazy for nothing. I want to be remembered, to be mourned, to be missed.*

That you are, Michele.

WAYFARER

Behind closed eyes Chuck heard a hum like the thrum of ship engines. The sound rose and ebbed, carried him back. Back to the smell, the darkness, the sea of bodies crammed into steerage sailing across endless gray. He sailed because his father, a man he scarcely knew, had summoned him to work in Gold Mountain. America, a place Chuck knew only in words. He was 12. He was scared. He was alone.

Chuck stirred in his bed, tried to escape the years. How long ago, that ocean crossing? How long did he wait, alone and afraid, on the dock for his father to meet him? Hours? A day? Uncle came to get him, take him to the place of work where his father was. Chuck tried to hear his father's voice. All he heard were ship engines. How long? How long before his father went back to China, left Chuck behind. Alone.

Chuck shifted beneath bed covers. Someone patted them into place, touched his hand. Chuck opened his eyes, saw an opaque sea of shadows. He tried to make out the features of the face bent close to his. She spoke, and he knew her voice. "Try to sleep, be at peace. You are safe."

The pump pushed breath into his body, Chuck drifted away. The drone in his ears grew louder, the waves rougher. He was aboard ship again. The sea raged. His stomach lurched. He was crammed among many again, all uniformed like him. His ship was one of thousands, hunter and hunted. The enemy burst into being in a ridge of green above high white cliffs. He watched days and nights break, flame. Their ship inched closer to the beachhead, barren, open, studded with white iron spiders. The waterline washed with flotsam. From the rolling deck, Chuck watched the onslaught, the slaughter. His insides shuddered. He was afraid, but primed. He was not alone.

Not that time. He knew the names of the men in his unit. During basic training he found a friend or two not too leery of serving with him, a Chinaman. All the guys of the half-track team came to depend on him, like he did them.

D-Day plus five, they landed. Their anti-aircraft unit roared ashore past the wounded waiting for evacuation, the bodies waiting for eternity. Their half-track vehicle dug tire tracks and tank treads into the soaked sand. Solid ground. The churning inside Chuck calmed. A high whine, a swooping dive started their ack-ack barking. The enemy plane strafed men darting between popping puffs of sand dancing all along Omaha Beach. Artillery bit glinting metal. The plane spiraled smoke. The half-track guys cheered.

A soft smile slipped into spent cheeks. Part of a team. A group acting as one. He might be scared, but he was safe. He belonged.

How long? How long did it last, belonging? The months ran together. The half-track rumbled across France, rolled into Paris for a week. They shivered through the Battle of the Bulge. A Belgian family invited Chuck for Christmas dinner. Goose, a taste of a tradition he didn't know. The family even wrote him.

The half-track rattled through Europe, moved between armies and divisions, went wherever their team was needed. Stood watch over anything that might be bombed, protected men and machines bent on defending or building bridges, like the one they crossed with the Seventh Army. They raced through Germany, stopped thirty miles outside Berlin.

That was the beginning of the end. Chuck was discharged. Nowhere to go. No place to live. No longer safe. Scared. Alone.

Somebody pushed the oxygen hum higher. Chuck rebelled against the noise whooshing in his ears, blotting out the war, the peace. Chuck opened sightless eyes. One morning he had awakened and couldn't see, so he closed his eyes, let the grayness carry him back to a time when everything was bright. How long lying there, suspended between wakefulness and sleep?

A voice he knew murmured. Mae kept watch. She alone knew his story. After the war, sleeping on tables shoved together in the restaurant where he worked during the day, worked hard to make his place in America. Finding success, losing it. She wanted to keep him safe. He knew she could not. Not this time. Chuck trembled. Scared. Alone.

Happenstance

Old habits die hard, mused George Lemain as he sat in Horatio's Café. The Cuban rum he savored brought back his days in the island constabulary when all things Cuban were forbidden and contraband.

George enjoyed his outings to Horatio's, a nexus for tourist and local alike. Jack Cabot, the pseudo pirate proprietor, knew how to attract the vacationer while retaining the regular. A chameleon, Jack Cabot from Kankakee. At one time Jack dealt in rum and cigars under the table. Now, he cultivated the latest crop of island denizen: refugees of questionable character.

Really, the new Council leading the island into the millennium was most adept and adaptable conceded George. Pity it took them so long to borrow the business model employed by more progressive Commonwealth islands. Indeed, the cottage industry of marketing citizenship-cum-passport had saved their island from the onus of bankruptcy and, worse, embarrassment.

George swirled the rum. Astute, to offer such a commodity in this day and age. Escape, legal and luxurious. For a price, of course. Everything came with a price. This, George noted with satisfaction, hadn't changed since he was an Inspector dedicated to maintaining laws, written and otherwise, in this small swatch of humanity. Now, instead of subterfuge and dissimulation, the miscreants were aboveboard, well heeled, versed in making money and in avoiding taxes. Legally, more often than not. Given the vetting the applicants underwent, such as it was, the likelihood of a mass murderer or a terrorist seeking safe haven on their island was minimal. Truly ingenious, this new breed of island administrator.

George's thoughts swirled, brought the image of the Commissioner, the combative bantam rooster who crowed with control or strutted on assumption. The Commissioner, his erstwhile superior, had also retired, though far less willingly than George. After all, George acknowledged, his own pension was comfortable, and well earned. He left the department driving the vehicle he had used for so many years under the Commissioner's myopic command. A generous retirement gesture in recognition of George's long, loyal and, most of all, discreet service. An exemplary Inspector. What did the Commissioner get? Indigestion, perhaps. George chuckled at the thought, then sighed. He did miss the thrill of confrontation.

A gaggle of new guests wandered into Horatio's, talking, flirting, intent on themselves. As expected, the women were beautiful, beckoning in beachwear if young, or bedecked with jewelry if of a certain age. The men were handsome in shorts or paunchy in loose shirts and blatant gold. Some, the fortunate ones, distinguished by white hair and trim torsos captured eyes, summoned smiles. Alas, women of that certain age rarely could count on nature to bless them with tempting tresses or smooth skin that didn't scream facelift. Pity, the unfairness of age and gender.

A younger couple, probably recent arrivals on a low fare flight or cruise ship, scanned the room festooned with fishnets and bright floats, spotted a space near George's table tucked in the corner. The girl slid onto the tall bar stool, braced a long leg on the crosspiece. A graceful gold anklet of flowers peeked from beneath her draped skirt.

An undercurrent of unease surfaced, much to George's surprise. What was it about her, this innocent smiling with the thrill of her first Big Vacation to the Caribbean that unsettled him? He directed his gaze to her escort. A man some years older, a trifle too practiced in his attentions. A professional? That nick, a thin slash, in the left eyebrow added a hint of the sinister. Eye color? George sifted through the colors he'd used in his reports of petty thieves and small time hustlers he had met in the past. Hazel, perhaps. Gray. Green. Evil.

George shook himself. Indeed, he must acquire a hobby. Something to divert his mind from the dark corridors of his onetime career. Trying to outsmart the criminal and the politician and still survive between the two had been exhausting, enveloping. And, apparently, mind altering. A diversion was in need. "Cricket, that's the ticket," George said quietly.

"Right!" Jack Cabot planted a bottle on the table. "Talking to yourself, Lemain?"

"No, I heard you coming. Do sit down, join me for a sip."

"What's this business? Cricket."

"Something to while away the days."

"Don't tell me you're already bored? On this beautiful island of sun, sea and loose morals?"

The tinkle of the girl's laughter slipped between the men, beckoned to George. A floral skirt flashed fast as a blink before his eyes. What was that? Too much rum?

"What about a refill?" Jack tipped the honey liquid into George's empty glass.

No, it wasn't the rum. Challenge quickened George's blood. Memory may have brought the blur to mind, but the notch in the eyebrow of the man at the bar summoned a specific scene, a troubling reminder of a task left undone. "To the innocents abroad." He clinked glasses with Jack, then drained his dry.

Jack stared. "In a hurry?"

"Yes, indeed. I have miles to go, places to see, or some such thing."

The black car sped down a familiar roadway, going back, miles back. Months back. With the vehicle sheltered under pandanus and palm, George Lemain retraced his steps along a narrow path to a pristine beach. On that distant day candy colored fishing boats bobbed on the dazzling blue horizon. Today, powerful yachts weighty with wealth and influence dominated the bay. His eyes dropped to a patch of sand. Soft. Pure. She had lain there, that young innocent. Long brown hair spread like a fan, floral skirt flared above splayed legs. The knife slit in her throat barely visible. That thin nick, so similar to the slim slit in a thick eyebrow shadowing an eye of shifting hue.

A pity, a true pity, George repeated. Dead, an innocent abroad. And he, Inspector George Lemain, swept up in the rapids of change in politics and policing had not unmasked her true killer. She deserved better.

George set the car in motion. Like a homing pigeon it sped across black stretches. Surely his old friends in the constabulary would welcome him, permit an old colleague to haunt his old haunts and, perhaps, just perhaps, examine files from a problematic period when a pretty visitor came ashore but did not leave and when a series of violent altercations flared among tourists. Indeed, one brawl resulted in a confiscated knife and a man being taken to headquarters, photographed. Fingerprinted. A formality, a mere formality, written in blood.

Yes, George Lemain mused, he might be able to give that girl on the beach her just due after all. Pity if he didn't.

CASTAWAY

Vernon balled tissue paper around the hard curves of the hanger. He draped the deep blue jacket over the padding, took care there were no creases in the back, no sag in the shoulders. Though old and no longer worn, the jacket meant much.

He hooked the hanger on the far end of the rod deep inside the closet, adjusted the sleeves to hang free. Sky blue hung against ivory. Minutes earlier Vernon had examined the lacy wedding gown in window light, searched for yellowing, then put away the dress so the folds fell into a semblance of his mother's figure. His niece remained strangely reticent to his offer to send the bridal dress for her own daughter's marriage. No response of any kind. Vernon could only shake his head. His brother Kendal was most remiss in failing to teach his daughter the manners and etiquette their mother had so painstakingly instilled in them.

Sunshine and clutter crowded the kitchen. Vernon eyed a large plastic box with a slit top sitting on the counter. His blue eyes squinted against the light, calculated how much spare change from his grocery runs filled the container. Close to a thousand dollars, he surmised, about as much as the last time he hauled the full box to the bank in Andrew's car. Andrew. What a godsend. A licensed, albeit inattentive, driver willing to chauffeur Vernon on errands in exchange for a full tank of gas and a cup of coffee. He would call Andrew, schedule a shopping trip with a stop at the bank first. Vernon would keep some cash for groceries and utilities, deposit the bulk into the checking account. Property tax was coming up.

Standing above the sink, Vernon sipped coffee. He watched a young man stride toward the house, then cross the street. Through narrowed eyes Vernon tried to identify which of the three newcomers to the neighborhood he was. One of the roommates was friendly. The other two had looked Vernon up and down, the snicker in their eyes dismissed him to the dustbin of the old and useless.

Vernon bristled at the recollection of that encounter. Where was the respect white hair once earned? At 90 he still believed in civility. He dressed like a gentleman: sports coat, pressed slacks, tie, polished shoes. Above all, he behaved like a gentleman, controlling his dismay, if not disgust, when hooligans with pants sagging to buttocks, language of the gutter, and behavior of savages shoved past him on the bus. And their horrid rap music replete with vulgar lyrics insulted his ears.

Vernon finished his coffee and dialed Andrew's number. There was no reply. Vernon went about his life: bus, bills, library. Vernon jiggled the lock open. I must oil the keyhole he told himself as he walked into the kitchen. He stared, silent as the light shining on the clean countertop. The plastic box of coins was gone.

He snapped his mouth shut. He hurried to the back bedrooms, surveyed the shelves of phonographs of his beloved operas, a few of the recordings were one of a kind. He ran his finger along the spines of first editions and original librettos. In a narrow closet squirreled between bookcases, he touched treasured mementos, Vera's fur coats—leopard, beaver, Persian lamb—and his own full-length mink. Still safe, still his.

He called the police, then Andrew's son, the handyman.

With a new lock and a new awareness, Vernon packed his mother's wedding dress in layers of tissue inside a clean box from the garage. Before leaving, he took stock of the living room. Every flat surface hosted bric-a-brac of ceramic, stone, and china. The tables themselves belonged to another era, one his mother favored. There was a single cushion free of piles of paper in the long and once elegant divan. He sat there to watch the boob tube, an item Kendal had hectored him into purchasing on one of his infrequent visits to his older brother.

Kendal never stayed more than a few days. Afterwards, Vernon would return to his study, resume the careful examination and placement of postage stamps, foreign and domestic. He was an avid collector. Racks lined with precisely labeled philatelic albums walled the room. Some of the issues were rare, quite expensive, exquisite in every detail.

When Vernon returned from mailing his mother's wedding dress he noticed something amiss. Two brass statuettes of Shiva were absent from the score of figurines assembled on the mantel. He inhaled, reconnoitered the living room, then went to the back bedrooms. He exhaled. His prized collections hadn't been disturbed. He notified the police once more. Once more, nothing came of it.

He set about foraging in closets, opening boxes in the garage. His call was cordial and brief. The couple would drive to his home tomorrow. Vernon ate his afternoon meal of yesterday's frozen breaded shrimp standing at the sink. He watched the street. He was under surveillance.

Vernon swept open the door. The couple from Sacramento examined each item, raved about the quality of the fur, the luxury of the silk, the excellent condition of the leather goods.

"My sister loved fine things," Vernon said. "We both shared similar sensibilities—an appreciation of the luxurious, the feel of fine fabrics, the refinements of style and line." He smiled, remembering Vera. "I suppose that should not be surprising. We were twins. The first twins born on Samoa. Our birth was the stuff of local lore. My mother cherished all the gifts the islanders brought at our birth." Vernon bit his lip. The keepsakes from Samoa had disappeared from the tool shed one afternoon. He found the padlock broken, the door askew.

Egregious insult compounded the injury of loss. The native artifacts were of little intrinsic value. His father, a military man, said so each and every time his mother lovingly packed them for shipment to their next post, but he did not forbid her from taking them along. Regardless of circumstance or situation, his father conducted himself as a gentleman, with courtesy and dignity. His was the example Vernon emulated when he put on his own uniform, worn with pride and resolve. Vernon's time in the military was one of his happiest.

"I'm sorry she passed away," the woman said, pawing the leopard skin coat.

"Thank you." Vernon winced. Vera's passing had been prolonged and painful, perhaps more so for him than for her. He had dealt with her house bills and medical care, first using her funds, then his own savings. Without his knowledge or his permission, the medical staff at the rehabilitation center transferred Vera in the stealth of night to a state facility out of reach by bus or train. Vernon telephoned her. Vera cried, a male orderly walked in as she was showering. She screamed. He laughed. Vernon called, complained to people who did not care. Then Vera's mind began to short circuit.

Kendal was of no help. Not once did he come to see his older sister or contribute to her expenses in those three long years. Yet Kendal had money and time to buy a motorcycle and a summer home in Missouri, bragged about the purchases to his older brother.

Vernon cleared a spot on the desk for a photo of the Golden Gate Bridge suspended between blue sky and blue sea. The captain who scattered Vera's ashes sent the picture with a handwritten note. It soothed Vernon to think his twin was wending her way back to their island birthplace.

Kendal visited after Vera died, chose the things of hers he wanted, instructed where they were to be shipped. Kendal's advice as he roared away: dump all that crap. Vernon stood on the threshold, watched man and motorcycle disappear.

The dumpster filled quickly. Thirty years of *National Geographic*, chronicles of vivid veracity rejected by the library, fell into oblivion. Glossy opera magazines thudded into ignominy. The tacky key chains from banks and former employers, the amusing giveaways at office parties and company picnics were discarded, like Vernon had been by people and firms.

Though his trips by bus were less frequent, Vernon continued his errands to bank and coffee house, library and doctors. He continued to lose items housed in his home. The losses were noted, but not notable. Not like the plastic box of coins. He learned to live with the knowledge he was prey. He didn't bother to call the police.

One afternoon, the mailman shouldered open the door to the garage, followed Vernon's shouts. Vernon lay on the floor, walled in by stacks of cardboard boxes. The mailman called 911, visited him in the hospital, bought a cell phone on his behalf and keyed in phone numbers. He had struck up a friendship with Vernon because of their shared obsession. The letter carrier combed estate sales and flea markets for antiques and collectibles, then resold them at garage sales. He knew about Vernon's collections.

Kendal came to the hospital. On the second day he left Vernon to fend for himself. Vernon went from hospital to rehabilitation, survived three agonizing weeks surrounded by the immobile, the incontinent, the incoherent. He hated what he saw, willed himself from a wheelchair to a walker.

Again, the mailman rescued Vernon, picked him up, brought him home. He came by before his rounds to help Vernon in and out of the shower and to open the door for the physical therapist. He came at the end of his rounds, handed Vernon his mail, and helped do what was needed. The mailman had the key to the house and everything in it.

Vernon kept possession of the checkbook, paid bills as they arrived. That evening, the postman obliged and rolled open the closet door. Vernon asked him to lift the cloth draping the blue jacket.

"Hey, is that your uniform?" the mailman asked. "Does it still fit?"

"Perfectly. I haven't changed a bit." Vernon propped himself up on the pillow. "Lock the door as you leave."

Once the latch clicked, Vernon picked up his pen, wrote the last two checks, read a letter from a dear and distant friend, then gazed out the window. Vernon watched the edges of day fade. He turned to the closet, looked at the blue sleeve, still straight and firm, all that was visible of his long ago youth. Vernon settled into crisp bed linens, closed his eyes.

SAME TIME, SAME PLACE

Volpina, the red haired fox, swept her silky tail through ragged grass. Sun, languid and low in the sky, caressed the meadow with a farewell kiss. Volpina trotted on a track she knew well. With mouth open, pearl teeth gleaming, she cut closer to a double row of parallel slats. Within a leap's reach of the fence, Volpina stopped.

At the appointed time, Galletto, a rooster of burnished red and gold sporting a fine red cockscomb, emerged from the lean-to. He stood, head high, neck robed in a thick iridescent ruff, legs stockinged in nubby yellow. With deliberate, high arched steps, Galletto strutted into Volpina's sharp gaze. He paused, lifted his shoulder-wings, tilted his majestic head and beaded a dark eye on Volpina beyond the verge. She raised a forepaw. Fox and rooster locked eyes. Then, with slow grace, Volpina settled on her slim haunches. Purpose propelled Galletto toward the perimeter of wood. Volpina rose to her feet, Galletto fluffed his ruff. Her mouth stretched wide, his wings stretched wide. Volpina lifted a paw, Galletto pointed his claws. She lunged, he flew. She was on the ground, he was on the fence. She sidled along the fence, he sidestepped atop the fence. Her red tail brushed the ground, his handsome wings fluttered the air. She moved left, he moved too.

A man appeared. He wore a black felt hat with a pointed peak, carried a battered flat pan. Volpina watched him approach. Galletto jumped into the dust behind the barrier. Fox and rooster exchanged glances, sent a message.

Mouth wide with glistening teeth, Volpina swept her fine red tail across stubbled stalks in salute. With his cockscomb reddening, Galletto lifted a clawed foot in farewell. Each understood. Tomorrow, same time, same place.

What We Call Life

MAXINE

Maxine slowed. Her silver chandelier earrings jerked with each thump. Then the danglers on her lobes swung in a circle as she looked over her shoulder, shimmied as she veered right. The tangerine Jaguar shuddered to a stop. Maxine let loose all of the swear words she'd picked up from six continents over six decades. Her tight blue eyes glared back at her in the rear view mirror. She scowled, then smiled. The cut and paste doc did a good job on her face. Then she spotted a baby blue junk heap edging into her space. Maxine cut the motor, hauled one leg in chartreuse tights, then the other from behind the wheel.

Hands on hips, Maxine frowned at the front tire, flat as last night's champagne. Dark red lips, fuller than nature made, compressed into thin disapproval. An over-the-hill dude strutted toward her, arms swinging loose like he owned her as well as the world.

"Looks like you got some trouble," Mr. Smug smirked.

"Nothing I can't handle."

"That right?" A black loafer looking for a shoeshine kicked the limp rubber.

"Don't kick what's not yours."

"Touchy, aren't you? Just trying to help." His belt cut deep as he bent over the tire. He fast-handed something, stood up. The hubcap clanged free, danced into the dirt. "Look at that! Just falling apart." Big teeth lined up in a grin wide as a road going to nowhere. "Maybe you better come along with me. Get you to a gas station." Mr. Smirk

157

leaned back on his worn down heels and eyed the over-dyed blonde. "Sign back there says fifty miles ahead."

"Wasn't there one ten miles back?"

"Station's there. What's left of it. Not enough business to keep it going." He grinned his best come hither leer.

Maxine narrowed her eyes as much as her tightened skin allowed. She jerked her head, her earrings went crazy. "Let me get my stuff." She popped the trunk, showed him her ample behind. She heard his cheap shoes crunching gravel. She rummaged faster.

"Here, let me give you a hand." He moved closer.

Maxine and her earrings wheeled around, her fist of diamond rings curled around a tire iron. "Not so fast, Daddio."

Double Negative

"Who's this?" Ginny pulled out a faded black and white picture shuffled among many in a shoebox.

My sister and I were sorting through the leftovers of a life just as we had for my mother fifteen years earlier. This time Ginny was helping me put order in my own. We stood in a room my mother had often visited, a nether world of possibilities, unlike the world outside with its hard light and harder facts.

Of a moment, my mother's voice, at once familiar yet distant, reminded me.

"Ma's foster mother." My eyes sidled sidewise to sneak a peek at Ginny's face.

"How do you know?" Ginny's eyebrows peaked in puzzlement, a look familiar from our growing-up days in Chinatown.

"Ma told me. You know, when we were home alone."

But we were in a new place when she had told me. Window sheers strained out sunshine, softened appearances, brought back the past. In half-light I turned to the door, watched shades of gray shape into a small figure.

"Hi, Ma. Been a long time."

"I know, Daughter." Her slow o stripped away the silence of separation. "Not so easy, not like before."

She drifted toward the photo on the desk, looked at the likeness of a woman. "Foster Mother. Immigration picture. Not young, not old."

A whiff of my mother's faraway home, sharp and stinging,

dusted with disappointment and salted with sorrow, rough-
ened my mother's voice.

"Old by the time you met her. Grandfather's funeral. Only
other person left in that house was my sister-in-law, the wife
of your Grandma's only son. Dead by then, too. It's not right,
burying a son."

"Gee, you remember back to the old house? You were
just a little kid." Ginny held the photograph straight as
a knife between fingers warped much like my mother's.

"It was later." I hurried my words to drown out the
echo of another conversation.

"I was the only kid at Grandma's. We all had to squeeze
around the table to eat. It wasn't much of a dinner."

"Big meal comes after the funeral, Daughter. No fancy food.
Simple soup, cold chicken, plain vegetables. Nothing sweet,
nothing red. Lots of salt."

Ginny's curiosity pulled me back. "Was it at the apartment, after me and Bit married, moved away?"

"I can't recall exactly," I lied.

Textured light threaded through sheers, patterned my
sister's face. The curtains at Grandma's had been textured,
too. Thick. Old.

"I don't remember much about the funeral. Did Grandma
even go?"

"Uh-huh. Wore a white blouse, black skirt. American style like
me and my sister-in-law. Each of us holding Grandma by the arm."

A side movement caught my eye. Ginny handed me
the picture of a neat woman: brow broad, eyebrows

precise, eyes unseeing, mouth noncommittal. I studied the oblong snapshot, marveled at all the shades of gray, the background of ash. Listened to the past.

"I remember I got a nickel wrapped in white paper, a brown chunk of raw sugar tucked in the folds."

"To chase away the taste of death, buy something sweet, Daughter."

The taste of salt again filled my mouth. "Did you notice, Ginny? Grandma's already dressed like an old lady and she's, what, maybe 35?"

"Looks like good material. Now we know where Ma's expensive tastes came from."

Behind Ginny's banter, the sunset shades of my mother's voice colored a scene only she knew.

"Silk, not cotton. Small flowers, yellowish white, greenish yellow woven right into the cloth. Always fancy things. Before the Depression."

A smile caressed my mother's cheeks into a child's. "But not as pretty as my own mother's dress—silk, smooth, shiny, soft. The color of pale melon. She came to visit me, came after they sold me, brought my baby sister along. That made me real happy."

Eyes shining, my mother stroked the air. Warped fingers played over fabric touched just once. "Beautiful."

Ginny stood between sunlight and shadow. "Ma got sort of tight lipped about Grandma later."

"Never saw my mother or sister again. Foster Mother wouldn't let me. Just her and me on the boat to Gold Mountain."

"That last visit to Cleveland."

Ginny looked at me. "What do you mean?"

"Remember? Ma went to see her sister-in-law, the only one still alive who knew about her home village."

"Now that you mention it, yeah, Ma wanted to find out so she could go back before she died, but for some reason the sister-in-law didn't tell her."

"Deathbed promise. Grandma made her swear never to name the village ever again."

Ginny shook her head, her hair still not gray. "If only Ma got to go home."

Soft as smoke, my mother's voice returned to me.

"Your life is made before you."

"Ma." Ginny sighed. "Seems she never said much about anything. Except maybe to you when you were too little to understand."

My mother and I, companions in silence, companions in loneliness. "No, I didn't understand much." Not even the last time.

"Do you remember your mother, your real mother's face?"

"Maybe not to see, but always to feel. You'll find out." My mother faded into half-light. "Don't cry, Daughter. I had my life. Live yours."

Ginny walked through a wedge of faltering day toward the doorway. "I don't know what you want to do with those old pictures. I suppose someone should keep them, someone who remembers. But, after us, who's going to care?"

Dusky blue blended into a gray darker than ash, but lighter than shadow.

YouTube

It started innocently enough. Mascagni's barcarole from *Silvano* on YouTube. But instead of shots of the full orchestra playing the opera interlude, scenes from *Raging Bull* filled the screen. Melody coupled with muscle conjured up other crossovers.

Connie Francis recorded an Italian favorite, "Violino Tzigano." The hit single crossed over to Italy. Teenagers in Rome bunched around the jukebox sang the lyrics exactly like Connie did, mispronouncing the Italian words *suona, suona* as *zona, zona* even though they knew better. Elvis was smarter. He changed the lyrics, singing "It's Now or Never" instead of "O Sole Mio."

Crossovers went both ways. Pino Donaggio's song, "Io che non vivo più di un'ora senza te" topped US charts as "You don't have to say you love me" which is not what his title says. Elvis added swivel and sass to this lover's lament breathy with pain.

Some crossed over free and clear. Mahalia Jackson needed no gospel translations. Nor did Ray Charles and "I can't stop loving you." The Platters were tops everywhere, toured Europe and crossed over to Italy, minor morality scandal in Ohio notwithstanding.

Which brings us to Buck Naked and the Bare Bottom Boys, a band less known for its rockabilly style than for its dress-less style. Buck Naked crossed over from Nebraska to the Castro in the early '80s. He wore a Stetson, pink cowboy boots, bone sunglasses, and a strategically placed toilet plunger. The plunger handle did not interfere with his guitar riffs. The backup guitar and the drummer were dressed for the most part, their bare bottoms only seen when they turned around to bow.

Like Elvis, Buck Naked changed crucial words, and so was born "Bend Over Baby and Let Me Drive" sung with lots of skin and swerve. From the stage Bend Over Baby crossed into an Electrical Engineering class to help describe the esoteric Return Ratio Method—testing an electronic circuit containing a signal source by displacing that source (bend over baby) and replacing it with another (let me drive)—in more visual and visceral terms. The concept and the vision graduated into industry, where a generation of analog engineers used the Bend Over Baby method in the lab.

Even the trio Peter, Paul and Mary crossed over, doing their part in complex filter circuits when three components changed roles (low pass, band pass, or high pass) to determine function and sound. But Buck Naked's crossover created a lasting impression.

All this because of YouTube, repository and purveyor of the past, the present, and the playful.

FREE

The book bag pulled Clovis's left shoulder down. Heat radiated off the cement apron fronting shops baking in late afternoon sun. A man behind the Frank's Construction Supplies window looked up when her body broke the screen of sunlight. Clovis straightened her back sheathed in a tee and lengthened the stride of tight jeans and sandals, walked the gauntlet of shops with elbow pipes, brick faces and fence samples.

No passerby would suspect that behind the storefronts another long flat building housed a single apartment bracketed by storage units assigned to the streetside offices. Clovis had heard about the two rooms from a fellow Arizonan. The rent was cheap, the bus stop two blocks away, the route straight to campus. The lodgings, up a few steps from the gravel yard, were quiet once trucks and cars vacated the lot. The kitchenette, an alcove off the living area, served her needs and the bedroom was adequate. All she really wanted was a way station to somewhere bigger and better. By all rights she should have been back in the desert scrabbling in the dirt for arrowheads like her parents, but she had left that life behind through luck and persistence. She accepted her place in the universe like she accepted this apartment.

At the window facing the rear doors of the businesses, Clovis reached to unlock the latch to air out the rooms. Before she could, a knife of humid air stabbed her hand. She examined the seam between frame and sill, looking for a telltale anomaly like she used to do when examining layers of sandstone. What she detected compelled her to look down. The ground beneath the window was unsettled. Clovis raised the window, leaned over the sill. Her brown eyes tracked the line of disturbance. An upended galvanized bucket stood close to the building, a splotch of dark soaked the dirt under the drainpipe. The bucket gleamed, a glint in the dark eye of earth.

Clovis slowly lowered the sash, went out and paced the stretch of locked back doors to the businesses facing her apartment. That night she sat in the straight chair at the table facing the window, opened a textbook while eating a sandwich. She moved to the wingback she'd bought at Goodwill, turned the armchair toward the window, and read. She turned out the light, moved to the window, wedged a narrow pipe into the side jamb, leaving only a slit open for air. Standing in the dark in the middle of the room, Clovis decided: I don't want to live like this.

Someone had moved the bucket from the drainpipe, poured out old rainwater onto dried out dirt, turned the pail over for a step up. A step up into her apartment.

The next morning Clovis made a stop on the way to campus. The pawn dealer sized her up before handing her the model she wanted. She answered his look with, "I'm a woman of the '80s. I know how to handle this. Where I come from, these are everyday." She left an arrowhead old as sand cliffs on the glass case.

Clovis reverted to routine. Classes, studying. Another wave of heat invaded the city. The temperature was like Arizona, the humidity wasn't. On the hottest night, Clovis lifted the lower sash higher than usual. The open window gave little relief, but it would free her. Of that she was sure.

She angled the armchair toward the glass panes staring at night, then sat on the dining chair positioned behind the wingback. From that seat she had a straight shot at the window. She shut off the light, let the darkness creep in.

She almost dozed off in the heat, but a rustle roused her. Wood slid against wood, silent and slow. The sash rose effortlessly. Unseen and unmoving, Clovis watched. Brown eyes shaped the dark into recognizable forms. Black gloves gripped the window frame. A black shoe, then a black leg reached over the sill. Quiet, the intruder hoisted the bulk of his body into the room. He did everything Clovis expected him to do. She did as she expected to do. He toppled to the floor.

The police carted him away. "I didn't want to live in fear," Clovis told them. "I'm alone out here. I bought the .38, just in case. It's registered. I'm licensed."

The police didn't press charges. Their report cited self-defense. They found a snap knife in his waistband. Clovis was free. Free to live as she wanted.

Promises to Keep

Malcolm grunted as he topped the outcrop and clambered onto the path to Than's house. The hand-hewn structure, built more for the eye than for the elements, blended in with trees and brush. He passed a goat tethered to a tree, the limits of its freedom outlined in a circle cropped clean of weeds.

"Welcome, Malcolm." Leviathan sat in a lotus position awaiting his visitor.

"Say, Than, you ever going to put in a real ladder so you don't have to play Tarzan to get to your place? People might think you're antisocial or something."

"If I were antisocial I wouldn't have provided a rope ladder." Leviathan rang a brass bell, " Nepi, please bring tea."

Nepi, a youth of dark hair, handsome eyes, and lithe frame appeared with a tray and a smile. He placed the salver on the low table before his master, Leviathan.

Malcolm watched the youth, maybe 16, glide soundlessly into the dark recesses of the makeshift house. He scowled. "He's growing up. What are you going to do with him, Than?"

Leviathan poured tea for them both. "Why, send him to Berkeley. When the time comes." He smiled, "I promised his mother."

"How's he going to get into Berkeley if he doesn't go to school? He's stuck out here in the middle of nowhere."

"Really, Malcolm, don't you think I'm erudite enough to educate him in every way? In addition, he has a tutor three days a week to train him in the ways of academia."

"What about being with kids his own age?" Malcolm stared into the tea. His breathing returned to normal.

"You know, I don't pass judgment. Your life is your life, but he's a kid."

"You're just jealous," Leviathan murmured. "Jealous because my talent, unlike your art, has been recognized. Recompensed." His pale eyes glanced at the small book bound in fine leather lying on a table designed for the foyer of an elegant home.

"Don't give me that! You just happened to write a nice blurb on a rich poet who was weird going on bonkers."

"That's mean spirited, Malcolm. As you very well know, his wife found my writing to her liking and she appointed me the protector of the poet's name and legacy. Of this, I have been most devout."

"Yeah, and she paid for your trip to the Far East to find the truth behind the poet's greatest and last poem. You just happened to find a boy along the way. A boy with a needy mother."

"You *are* jealous, Malcolm!"

Malcolm snorted. Tea sloshed onto the saucer.

"It was a contract, a legitimate contract, and I fully intend to uphold my end of it. Nepi will receive a formal education. He will be integrated into society. How he chooses to live his life after he enters the outside world, your world Malcolm, will be for him to decide. Coercion is not the way to enlightenment and self-knowledge."

"Will you put in a metal ladder after he leaves?"

"Time will tell, Malcolm. Now, drink your tea before it grows cold. Let's enjoy each other's company."

Nepi hovered in the background laying flower petals on a golden rug.

Loss

Jim stared at the mirror in disbelief. "It was here yesterday," he said aloud to his razor. "It's got to be here." He capped a meaty hand on his scalp, rubbed his pate like a lamp and hoped the genie called Hair would appear. Nothing. Nada. Zilch. Zero.

"What happened? Where did it go? It was here last night," Jim bellowed to the looking glass. The medicine cabinet door squealed at his rough handling. Nope, Hair was not hiding inside. "Damn!" Medicine shelves of ointments and tubes of gel jumped at Jim's grand slam. A hubbub of hard knocks hammered inside the bathroom. Cabinets and drawers got a working over, but nobody snitched on Hair's whereabouts. Jim even got onto his knees to look under the sink, a dark and mysterious place littered with black flecks. Jeez, did he have rats? Sneaky freeloaders. Jim kicked the wastepaper can right on the Good to the Last Drop slogan. The coffee can crimped in pain. Well, one sure thing, the mice weren't hanging around Hair. Jim pounded the sink, pounded his head. "Where are you, Hair?"

He stormed the bedroom, attacked the bed with thumps and tosses, shouted, "You can run, but you can't hide!" Top of the dresser, under the bed, closet floor, inside places and spaces he hadn't checked since Mabel moved on. Jim shot up straight. Mabel. It was Mabel! That blonde floozy with loose screws must have come slinking in when he wasn't home, took Hair just to get even. Heck, what was he saying? The locks, he changed the locks. Though he wouldn't put it past her to hook up with the locksmith just to get the key. There were only fifteen locksmiths listed in the phone book.

Jim stood in the middle of his living-dining-TV area. Thick and sturdy like a lighthouse capped by a bright bald spot, Jim swept blinking blue eyes over the crinkly, smelly, unwashed jetsam of his daily life. "Hair, where are you?"

Off the shoulder of the armchair lounging against a corner of cobwebs and stale corn curls, a wavy swatch of flawless brown hair rested where it had landed. Snug as a bug in a rug, Hair flexed, as much as something soft and supple can flex, its carefully combed waves into a Mona Lisa smile. "You know what they say," the toupee said to the rug, "hair today, gone tomorrow."

THE MILL

No surprise did I show when Arnaldo knocked at my door. Not with him being a neighbor. Lived across the street in the home he built near a row of houses he put up touching shoulders like hens set to roost in a coop.

He stood on the veranda next to the birdcage, afternoon sunlight warming his back. Once was, on days bright like that one I'd be out in the fields handling the scythe. Back when I was young, back between the wars and even after. Then me and mine moved to this house built by me and my sons with Vigiuta scrimping and saving in every way. Built with hard work and music making. Generous, GIs were, with food and tips in those times of want and war.

But strange it was, Arnaldo standing at my door. My ears had heard the voice passing through flapping lips about him. His business. Made his living tearing down old things, putting walls where fields once were. Raising new walls the color of dead grass where old white ones stood for generations. Him, the one to batter the mill, the old home of us Mulinar, to make way for condominiums clinging to the soil like mushrooms on the face of a dead tree.

Before the first blow the voice rippled among the oldtimers, rumbled against pulling down the mill on the Viarsa, the house of the three miracles. The voice rose like the Viarsa once did when rains were strong and the riverbed twisted and turned. But the voice came to nothing like the sluggard Viarsa now, channeled straight and slow, confined between concrete arms.

So Arnaldo pushed his big machines against the mill, smashed the low room where once the waterwheel churned at the Viarsa's fitful will, the room where the great millstone ground corn into meal before the Great War cracked it, leveled the barn beneath the hayloft where a lightning bolt skipped over sleeping children to strike dead the horse in a stall below. A miracle, the villages said.

Arnaldo then crossed the courtyard to crush the sty where Delia raised piglets to sell to pay for her simple needs, tore out the faucet bringing village water to the courtyard, uprooted the walnuts shading the mill, but the poplar planted by my son was cut at the administrator's command into planks for his son's wedding bed.

Delia, the last Mulinar to live in the mill. Lived there even after a devil wind ripped the tiles from the roof above her bed. Lived there through a winter with only a black tarp between her and the stars. Lived there even though the estate administrator tried to drive her out and force her to move to this house, knowing me and Vigiuta had set rooms aside for her. But the angry talk and hard stares of villagers shamed him, made him release the estate funds he held tight as if his own to pay for new roof tiles, red against blue.

Delia lived in the mill even after City Hall sent her word sharecropping was no more. And gone, too, was the sharecropper's right to live free in the landowner's house—the mill. The village priest blessed those trying to push Delia out, but my sister he did not bless.

Stayed, Delia did, in the only home she ever knew. Lived there with the help of Don Davide. He came from a nearby village to console and counsel her. Gave Delia the name of a lawyer, a Communist. Stood up for the mill and the Mulinar, that lawyer. And won.

So Delia lived in that tall white house on the Viarsa keeping the old ways, keeping the story of the Mulinar and the mill of old alive. Wanted to end her days there, but even in this Delia was denied.

Took time, the killing of the mill. In the end, those of City Hall, castle and church bent and twisted laws, calmed grumbling villagers.

Arnaldo, now, belonged to the right party, the one favored by priest, mayor and administrator. Christians they called themselves, those fascists who added Democrat to their party name to fool the poor and the weak like men of their kind always do. No wonder it was Arnaldo to smash the mill into the dust of yesterday for the gain of today.

Six years, maybe more, after Delia was gone, fresh walls sprouted where my sister once lived. A rash of apartments covered the place where Delia and me were born, where my sons were born.

Now Arnaldo stood tall in the sun just as the mill once did. Polite, he was, saying all but one of the condominiums was sold, the one with a view of the Puint di Lanza, that bump of a bridge just a rifleshot away from the mill. The only rooms where a piece of the old mill wall still stood buried beneath plaster and paint. The wall scarred with three scabby bullet holes left by Serb marauders shooting at my young son. The white wall holding the entrance to the mill, the home of generations of Mulinar.

Arnaldo stood at my door, the blue of his shirt as blue as the sky behind. Offered that leftover piece of the mill to me and my sons, offered it at a price lower than the cost of the making of it. Saying we were neighbors, saying he knew it was where the Mulinar once lived. Saying it was a favor.

Behind his polite words, I knew. Knew his business was dying, dying slow like Delia. Knew he was saving his skin. Knew, too, the oldtimers kept my sister and the mill alive, telling and retelling stories of the house of the three miracles and of Delia, the last Mulinar.

Polite, I was. Wrong, it would be. A wrong against my sister and her memory, I said. And I closed the door.

Common Ground

Mauro stood straight, let the words wash over him. Gisa faced forward, intent on the ceremony. Both wore suits somber in color. Others had done what they had done with the same consequence. But unlike others, Gisa had insisted. Unlike others, Mauro acquiesced. So they stood together facing the priest. Just them, and those to bear witness. Mauro and Gisa walked down the aisle to the church door. Remilda, the matronly maid of honor, kissed Gisa. Mauro's best man and best friend clapped him on the shoulder, shook his hand in reassurance. Mauro escorted Gisa to a small house buried in green on a hill so small the villagers nicknamed it Piculit, Tiny. He stood at the threshold as she stepped through the door. Then he turned his back, walked away.

Like many, theirs was a marriage of inconvenience. Six months later, Gisa gave birth to the inconvenience. She named the boy Alvise, a name she had heard in her uncle's tales of long ago. Her uncle was dead, as were her parents, but Gisa managed. She worked at the cotton mill, the tiny house was hers. Mauro had a job at the steel mill, a willing worker with a strong back and a stronger will. He was not known to gamble or drink. Steady as an ox under the yoke.

Mauro was a man like other men, and Gisa was a woman like other women. What had passed between them had faded like the promise of spring before an arid summer. They went about their lives, separate and solitary.

Remilda tended the baby, watched the boy grow, go to school. She was paid more with the child's smiles than by his mother's money. From time to time Mauro bicycled to the Dopo Lavoro on a Saturday, passed the playing field, spotted a boy with blond hair and lanky legs running. Running to where?

When money was short for new shoes or medicine for whooping cough, Gisa would find a knot of waxed brown paper tucked behind the window shutters. A habit left over from the days of courtship. Wrapped tightly inside were enough lira notes to help her through. She never knew how Mauro knew. An upright and honorable man, Mauro. Correct to a fault.

Remilda sometimes bicycled to a farm at the edge of the village. Mauro rented a room in the courtyard. She stopped to exchange a few words with the women as the menfolk trickled back from field or mill. Sometimes she mentioned how well her charge Alvise was doing in school, how big he was. Mauro wasn't always there to hear. Remilda grew older, as did Alvise. He attended liceo in Guriza, the high school for local villages. Did well.

Alvise wanted to go to the military academy far away. A scholarship helped, but there were other expenses from time to time. Somehow Mauro knew. A wad of lira notes would be wedged between the shutters of Gisa's little house.

Months grew into years. Labor at the steel mill was loud, hot, gritty. Steel proved stronger than Mauro. Some of it sifted into his breath, settled into his body. Mauro lay between clean white sheets, grateful to see the bright sun locked outside the hospital window.

One morning of sunny blue, Mauro heard a murmuring of surprise grow among other patients as brisk steps neared his bed. He turned his dark eyes to see a tall, straight young man at his feet. The muted blue of his uniform highlighted the blondness of his hair.

"Buon giorno, Signor Zanon. I am Alvise Zanon, your son."

The silence of decades stood between the men. Both upright, honest, dutiful—their common ground. Father and son made peace.

RED

To hear the women tell it, that night of story was like no other. Laughter rang out on many a Saturday evening when women's tongues fanned faster than did playing cards. So raucous their voices grew the deaf sprouted ears to hear. First whispered from wife to sister, mother to daughter, the tale grew grander with each telling.

Such tales as this always begin on a lonely road leading from the dark into the dark. Black it was, black only as night can be, the earth shivering with cold and the sinking moon sucking the damp from the land. First one, then another oil lamp flickered in the hills beyond the village. Farm women rose, dressed, and rode their bicycles, cold as the grave, along dirt tracks, dodged puddles and ruts to the gravel path. In the village, one by one, wives of tradesmen and shopkeepers joined them. Pedaled, each did, to earn enough to buy what they did not have. For farm wives, a bit of sugar or a piece of cloth. For village wives, fresh vegetables or a bit of meat.

Once past the last house, the women exploded. Sang, those women. Loud enough to scatter the stars, shake fear out of the shadows. Shushing bicycle tires slurred through mud and over stones. Voices chorused, sang of love, courtship.

An hour or more it took to pedal to the cotonificio. The cotton mill stood across the bridge on the Isonzo. Stood there when Mussolini grew strong and still stood there when the Allies arrived.

That night, like always, the women passed Ofelia walking fast on the grassy track. No bicycle did she own, nor was there one to borrow. So she used what she did own: her feet. Carried her shoes to save them from wear. "Better walk than want," Ofelia said, "better fed than not." Washed her feet, put on her shoes at the factory door. Did that six days a week, Ofelia. So did the other women, their bicycles propped against the cotton mill at 5:00 each morning save Sunday.

But that night of story was unlike others. The women rode like always, then one, then another gasped, slowed and dropped right foot to the path, dragging a dusty trail. Ahead lay something unexpected. Unexplained.

A long tongue of fire writhed in the darkness ahead, writhed like the dead rising on judgment day. Never did a flame flare so ghostly, a changeling in the shifting gloom before dawn. So strong was their surprise, none could utter a word. Imagine that, if you can.

On a hidden hillock a figure rose, its shape knit from shadows of the night. A carbide lamp swung unsteady in a raised hand. The lantern's orange flame twisted, embraced a face with a sickly glow. A leer, a flash of teeth gaped wide. A voice rang out. A man it was. And such a man he was. Hair red as fire flared above a long narrow head, skin colored like rotting teeth, eyes bloody as the devil's. "Look."

The women released a breath, settled onto bicycle seats, skirts brushed tire guards. A man he was, no matter how ugly. A man not to be feared, not with him being one and them being many.

He ogled the women. "Watch," he rasped, tone husky. He lowered the lamp, its long licking tongue curled, exposed a pillar of red desire. "The wife, she was in no mood.

Watch. That's all you need do." His voice hoarse with want slithered like a snake among the women.

"Watch!" Giovanna exclaimed. "Oh, go on! As if I don't get enough at home." She shoved her weight forward. "Who has time for this?"

The lantern wavered, the red pillar drooped. Gleaming eyes faded.

A chorus of huffs gave way to a crescendo of rubber crushing earth. Before pedaling down the slow slope to the river Isonzo, Giovanna twisted around, saw nothing but darkness behind. The women burst into song, cruised into another day.

The night after the women whispered and wondered when they neared that hillock hidden in shadow. Slowed as one to see better. Disappointed they were, if truth be told. No man with glowing red eyes and flaming hair held a flickering beacon high for them to see.

But reappeared again, that ugly man ripe with desire, whenever cards were dealt and rumors traded. The women's laughter brought back that red shadow-man under the stars, lusty lamplight beckoning bright.

THE FIELD

The field ahead was yellow, vibrating with insects. The air smeared with dirty heat. A wide silver band of metal curved against the brown dirt road. The red scooter buzzing like a wasp slowed to a drone, sputtered. The riders, a man and a woman, tilted into the guardrail. A thick silver bolt carved a red curve into his knee.

Hot air flowed beneath and above her flying body. Her head cracked like an eggshell, a jagged red line etched the black behind closed eyes. They opened to a sky throbbing with yellow light. On all fours she searched parched grass, found a still body. Blood red sunbursts erupted in sun browned skin. The noise of the unseen floated in a shimmering cloud, colors blurred into a single shade of fear. A quiver, then a moan. No, not red splatters of death, but blood flowers of life falling from her head, watering the tanned body, bringing life anew.

Say What?

Kevin took the first forward facing seat, settled in next to a broad woman with short cropped hair, no makeup, and a business suit cut to fit a sergeant major. He stretched his left leg against the empty side seat—his sciatica was acting up—unlocked his briefcase and let BART carry him away.

There was a low chuckle, a finger tapped his knee. "Fancy meeting you here. Guess I'm a lucky bastard."

Kevin looked up into a pair of furious brown drills boring into him.

"Thought you'd get away, didn't you? Thought I wouldn't keep my word, didn't you, you sonofabitch bastard."

"Say what?" Kevin eyed the stranger. *A nutball, and he has to sit by me.* "You talking to me?" His eyes side shifted. *All the seats taken.*

"Don't you remember me? How could you forget Clint Wiley? One of the best in the IT department until we had a chat. You ass licking pencil pusher."

"Oh, you're out."

"No thanks to you."

"Not my fault you were a guest of the state." Kevin gasped. He saw muscles tense in the knotted hand grabbing his lapel.

"You're leaning on me." The sergeant major glared at both of them from behind her newspaper.

"Sorry. Just overjoyed to see my buddy here, the guy who canned me from my job."

Sergeant Major directed a long look toward Clint, took in his curdled grin, bad haircut, worse manicure, and tacky shirt and jacket. Then she turned a baleful gaze on Kevin. He refused to wilt. She dropped her eyes to the fisted lapel until Clint's hand began to unwind. Snapping the *Business Report*, she returned to reading an article about Bay Area layoffs.

"I got fired because of you."

"I share your pain," Kevin grimaced. "See, my resume. I got my walking papers last month. Fact is, I'm on my way to outplacement. Same outfit that handled you. How were they?"

"Are you shitting me?"

"Hey, downsizing whittles tall, short, big, little, IT and HR just the same. You know that's why you got let go. It wasn't me and you know it. It was economics. Robbing Peter to pay Paul, and I'm not Paul."

"No, no-no-no, you don't get off so easy. It was you. Somebody had to choose the ducks to pop, and you put in your two cents just because I hassled you a little. Couldn't take it, could you? Had to get even, didn't you? You ass licking asshole."

"You're repeating yourself there. And if you think my say-so could tank you, tank anybody, then you're giving me a lot more credit than the ones who tanked me did."

"And what about my wife?"

"What about her?" Kevin could smell cigarettes and coffee and something sour and old on Clint's breath. Kevin's hand cupped Clint's fist squeezing wrinkles into his suit.

"What are you doing?" Sergeant Major's voice was loud, and peeved. Heads turned, one commuter hunched lower in her seat and raised the volume on her headset.

"Just having a heart to heart with my old buddy here. What's it to you?"

"Keep it down. You're not the only one here." Sergeant Major rattled the paper menacingly.

"No, no I'm not. I've got asshole here."

Clint's head resumed normal proportions when he got it out of Kevin's face. Clint lowered his hardwired body in slow motion. "I lost her."

Kevin's eyelids fluttered. Lost her? Sergeant Major was still sitting on his left, big as life. Justice. The Women's Movement. Then his lids calmed down. "Oh, you mean Lucrezia, your wife. I'm sorry. Have you reported her missing?"

"Fuck you!" Clint half-rose, then settled down for the count. "Look you, it's all your fault. I lost my position, my self-esteem."

"Yeah, prison can do that I guess."

"I ought to take that scrawny neck of yours and snap it like a pencil, that's what I ought to do."

"Right, you mentioned that. You were pretty explicit in your message."

Clint chuckled, "You got it, huh?"

"One of the last pieces of official business to cross my desk before my...release from the company." What a great farewell, that envelope sitting in his In box on the day he got the news he was history. Thirty years evaporated in fifteen minutes with a guy half his age with half his experience and twice the ego. "But you shouldn't have printed your little note on the envelope for everyone to read."

"Why not? Everybody ought to know what a lying, conniving, opinionated asshole you are. You deserve fame."

"Well, maybe, but the message caused a tizzy with the postal service."

"Who gives a shit about those stamp collectors?" Clint sat back, shoulders taut.

Kevin could hear the crinkle of newsprint snapped in half. "Well, they notified the FBI. Your letter arrived at my desk inside a plastic pouch imprinted with the notification that, according to some postal code, mailed threats were handed over to the Feds before delivery."

Amazing how long a sneer takes to work its way across the lips to the corners of the mouth and up to the eyes.

"Of course, if they had contacted me, contacted me in an official capacity, I'd have to tell them what was on file. How Lucrezia, the company's top number cruncher, missed work at crunch time, then showed up wearing huge sunglasses because of a beaut of a shiner, courtesy of her husband, one Mr. Clinton Wiley."

Murder muddied Clint's even features, his hands balled.

From the corner of his eye, Kevin saw a white flag drop. The newspaper landed with a slap on Sergeant Major's lap. He had her undivided attention. "Now, you, me and this young lady," Kevin nodded to Sergeant Major, "know the whole story." And right on cue just as he'd counted on, the train started a slow screech.

"Opp, my stop!" Kevin leaped to his feet, his briefcase blocking Clint's rising body. With paper in hand Sergeant Major tailgated Kevin merging into the commuter horde surging to the exit. Kevin turned his head, "Gotta go! Outplacement."

Clint fought his way through the crush just as the train doors slid shut. Kevin was already on the escalator up, patting out the wrinkles in his suit.

A Day in the Life

Shark pumped his fist inside his right pocket. Slouch-walking down the gum-tacked sidewalk, he slammed a sneaker onto a tilted slab pitched into a dead brown patch of dirt. What that old woman want, he muttered. Getting on me for what I can't help.

His left hand fumbled in a slit of fabric, found purchase. Coins in hand, he jammed up against passengers boarding a bus, beaded his eyes into a dare to answer the driver's unspoken question, you a student?

Son of a bitch. Don't I look like one, he snarled into his mouth. A pair of glazed sunglasses glared at Shark as he shoved through a tight slot between standees. The hard eyes in the reflected image were knowing, the mouth mean. Shark nodded. The driver was right. Shark was past young.

He hopped buses until the transfer ran out and the city stopped. Buses had eaten up hours, churned through waves of accents, shed bad beginnings until the last one disgorged him at the end of the line. The parking lot was steaming with motor coaches, unlocked cars. A gaggle of goggle-eyed tourists pointed fingers and trained cameras over a cement wall. Shark joined them.

Paying big money to come see that? A hunk of steel colored like Josefina's hair. Who she fooling? Don't belong nowhere, that head. Shark watched the watchers, listened. They can't talk right either. He turned to the glistening row of late model cars. But that don't matter for them.

A skinny kid in sagging shorts with a skinnier girl in Capri pants pulled out a cell phone from a deep pocket, cuddled the pony-tailed girl and aimed the phone toward them, the bridge behind. They giggled at the picture, walked while watching themselves in the viewfinder.

Shark smirked, sauntered with long, low-slung steps to their place, swung a slow look around, then dropped a hand to the sidewalk, moved away. Shark cradled a fist in his right pocket, then did what he had never done before: crossed over.

"Where you going?" the driver asked.

Shark repeated the name the hunched man ahead of him mentioned. Shark held up a crumpled bill. A woman, wrinkled face brimmed in wide white cloth, pulled out a thin black wallet, edges worn gray, and carefully counted the singles twice before handing him five frayed ones for his found five. He fed the fare box, got a transfer. When he neared, the old lady looked up from under her hat brim. He shot her a short nod, she smiled.

Shit. Look at those eyes. Like Mother Green's. All the kids at the home said she could see right through the layers, the lies, down to where you lived. Not natural, green eyes clear like water.

Shark pimped down the aisle, caught the glance of a pale underfed blonde. She shifted her too smooth face to the window, planted a red Macy's bag onto the aisle seat. A heavy bracelet jangled as her arm squeezed a leather handbag closer to her side. He slowed, farted.

Shark, arms draped across the last row of seats, sprawled one leg down the riser. He watched a parade of young males neatened up for work sit in the midsection while shriveled grannies, blocking the aisle until coin purses were fumbled away, clambered into the front seats.

A stout mother hauling a folded stroller, child on hip, sat by a teen slouched against the window. A big man with a strong smell and a splotched backpack made his way toward him. Shark tensed, eyes slitted. That's right, you big bucket of shit, squeeze in next to that big ass mama. He strangled a laugh.

Maids, waiters, homeless, and a couple of short hair bitches. Washed out looks, washed out clothes. Nothing you can latch on to. Shark snickered. Except one thing. His right hand slid into his pocket, balled into a fist. No different over here.

He tailgated the bony shopping bag broad. She turned her fake face, shot a dirty look over her shoulder. What you looking at? Shark eyed the lobster claw clasp to thick gold links chained around her skinny neck, got a whiff of something. He scowled. Stinks like Macy's.

As soon as the stocky mother maneuvered the stroller off the bus, the bleached bag of bones took off across asphalt. Another green and white bus roared into the slot ahead, drew a crowd of white T-shirts and black hair from a roofed bench. Shark stood in the sun, spun a deliberate circle and long-legged into shelter shade. Let's see what comes along.

Voices jarred Shark awake.

"So where's the bus? Dad will be furious. It's all your fault, Adrienne."

"Oh, come on, you thought he was cute, too."

Shark took it all in. Sweet, real sweet. She's got her ass hanging out of those shorts, asking for it. Tits there for the taking.

Dusk and the bus came together. Shark took his time coming up from behind. He watched the seam of

Adrienne's shorts tighten, her hand in a pocket. Cotton pulled up, showed the sly smile of a firm cheek. Shark swore under his breath. Hey, baby, how about a nice fat finger up that fancy ass of yours fanning my face?

Change clanged into the fare box. The driver turned on the interior lights. "A quarter more." Adrienne squealed, her friend groped inside a patterned purse. Shark stepped aboard, flashed the expired transfer, moved fast past the driver eyeing Adrienne's breasts beneath a V-neck.

It was dark when he followed the girls off the bus into the parking lot. Headlights flashed, the pair got into a car. Shark walked into Longs, paced between racks of toilet paper and canned goods, looking busy, looking to see. It didn't take long to find her, one hand on the cart, the other holding a list, shoulder bag slung behind her, flap yawning open. Dumb bitch.

By the time the last feature was over all the mall doors except one were locked. Shark headed to the men's room but a janitor stood guard so Shark did his business and left. There were no more buses. He probed a pocket for the last bills from the woman's wallet he'd tossed into the food court trash.

Shark crossed a wide intersection, walked past shop windows and stragglers, bought a bottle before the clerk locked up. He found a bench deep in a bend under some trees. Shit, noisy as hell. Damn bugs. The liquor kept him warm but gave out too soon. Shark started walking, hugged bushy dividers, skimmed flat patches, skirted sightless houses lost in midnight sleep.

Shit, shit, shit, he muttered, racing to keep up with his heart. A corner street lamp cast a spotlight onto a sprawling two story, white in the night, the steep front yard studded with red and yellow, a squat fence separated private property from public. Easy living this side of the bay, no bitching old woman cutting you down, squeezing your balls for nothing.

Out of nowhere he heard Josefina's shrill voice hammering him down. Shark tightened a fist into a ball, pumped air.

A door slammed, a squeal chased by a low laugh fell down the hill. Adrienne's tight ass sashayed ahead of him, smooth white legs sliced into shadow. Fucking shit. That her? All by her lonesome? Sweet, real sweet.

Shark slid through darkness, fast, silent. He heard it before he saw it. Headlights crept around a curve, inched toward him. He stepped back into hedge gloom. A pale streak, slick in street light, arced. The newspaper fell short, lay in the gutter. The hand brake ratcheted, the car door opened. Low beams snared a flitting figure, cast a halo on pale hair. As she stooped for the plastic newspaper sleeve, an arm pinned both of hers against her chest, a hand aborted her scream. She flailed, but Shark held strong, dragged her into black night. He was in control.

Shark heard a hiss, a sleek shape leapt past his head. Porch lights snapped awake, exposed the unseen. Green eyes, clear as water, looked up at him. They followed him as he grabbed at long streets with long strides winding deep and dark into unknown places.

Hard Sell

Showered, shaved, pumped up for the public, Jackson Charger checked the car trunk, ticked off all he needed. Next buy, GPS. Cheapo company, not giving GPS to the field. Correction, part-timers. Once he made quota, he'd get the best. And more.

Five minutes late, not bad. Considering. Map was unclear where their street dead ended. Jackson composed himself, ran through the company routine, then swept a big hand free of restricting rings across a wavy mane. Gave him grief when he was too young for white hair, but it suited him now. Tall, six-six. Still straight. Big shoulders. Commanding. Like Moses. Charlton Heston before the NRA and Alzheimer's.

The man answering the door fit the faded voice on the phone. Jackson gave his best nod, threw in the lopsided grin. The guy was lean, spry, sported ear hardware and a chained cross. Another sucker. Know your client, the company manual said, and Jackson lived by the book. Except on weekends.

Jackson stood in the kitchen doorway a half second longer just for effect. He and his fluffed up hair nearly grazed the doorframe. Imposing. Especially for the wife, a runt foreigner. Bug-eyed, she stared like he was Jesus on the hoof. Familiar looking, but all foreigners looked alike, particularly her kind. Like cockroaches. Pretty soon they'd have the run of the country. Unless you took control. Heston drew the line at assault rifles, Alzheimer's does strange things.

Jackson sat where they wanted him at the kitchen table. He did the chitchat bit to build trust, then rattled off the spiel. "RGB Construction has grown exponentially since inception," he jabbed at the report inside a sheet protector. "RGB is moving west, pioneers in the building trade. Not just frame and foundation, but siding and roofs." Lumps just sat there. The old fart probably couldn't hear a gunshot and she probably didn't understand.

"And we do decks. I see you have one right above the patio door." Jackson also saw the Jesus Saves banner framing a moony-eyed JC. "Let's go outside and I can give you a visual inspection, warn you about future problems. The inspection and estimate are free, part of our all inclusive service."

Come on, come on, get a move on, you rattlebone skeleton, Jackson snarled behind stretched lips as Mr. Fart fumbled into garden shoes. Mrs. Fart stuck to the back like wallpaper.

Jackson ratcheted up the lop- to his side smile, pointed up to the deck. "See the cracks between the slats? Rain comes right through, soaks the chairs you set out. Avoid all that by lining the deck with waterproof flooring. No more cracks, no more leaks. Better yet, redo the entire deck with our weather resistant planking and, bingo, no more maintenance. You're home free." Bug-eyed, both of them. Damn, he was good. Jackson launched into manual Lesson Five.

"Now that shingle looks pretty bad. Dried. Faded. Costs a fortune to replace. If you go for RGB siding you fix it forever. No paint, no sealant, no nothing. Just let us work a miracle for you. Brought lots of samples to show."

Back at the kitchen table Jackson looked earnest. "Like I said, RGB is new to this area and because you responded first, you've been chosen. That's right, the first house in the neighborhood to have a total RGB makeover. And at a serious discount! Don't get me wrong, you might be the first offered this great deal, but I can't hold it for you long. The next client might snap at the chance of a near brand new home. If they do, you're out. You understand? Now, will RGB work for you?"

Jackson waited. Could almost hear the Farts' squeaky wheels turning. Turned the wrong way, it turned out, but he followed the book and said, "Sure, think about it."

Jackson sat back, put his own version of Lesson Seven, have a backup plan, into play. "Let me tell you, I'm only working for RGB until my own company gets going." He whipped out a business card. "Me and my partners are setting up a theme park. A Christian amusement park." Jackson nearly sniggered. Christian got them every time.

"Not done yet, but we already got rides, games, animals, food. How about a family pass for four people? Worth six hundred dollars. Yours for only sixty. A Christian place where good people like you can have good fun. A place to take the grandkids. Isn't that worth something?"

Dahlia's Fall

Mildred Trusdale stopped dead. Dahlia Livingston, her best friend, lay moaning on the salt and pepper runner. Her less than lithe torso twisted into the S-curve favored by Baroque beauties of some girth. "Dahlia, what happened?"

Dahlia artfully tilted her head to peer up at the hovering shadow. Thick lashes batted big browns. "Oh, Dred," she whispered, "nothing." Dahlia smiled bravely, turned to look into the midnight blue eyes of the man on one knee at her side. "Really, nothing."

Dred followed Dahlia's gaze, snapped to attention. That head of coffee colored curls, bulging biceps, tattoo bursting out of a tight T-sleeve triggered alarm bells. The Hunk of Engine 39. Dred stepped back, admired the tableau. Dahlia's dingy blonde hair, currently streaked with gold, framed her pale face like a tarnished halo. Hot pink spandex sheathed her gently bent legs, a matching halter top peeked from beneath a cleverly cut black overblouse with a deep V-neck, teasing without revealing unsightly bulges.

"Let's make sure. We can take you to the hospital for examination." The Hunk's voice washed over Dahlia like a soothing wave. Dred folded her arms, let herself go with the flow.

Dahlia raised a limp hand, sturdy pinky poised like a ballerina. "Oh, no, no, that's not necessary." She latched her big browns on The Hunk's face, square jaw and all, and fanned her lashes with hurricane force. "See!" Dahlia arched a thick foot, toenails polished the same pink as the stretched spandex. "I can bend my ankle. Oh, a twinge or two, but nothing I can't bear." Silver clogs nearly blended into the regulation gray gym rug.

Dred dropped her arms. Clogs? Dahlia's wearing clogs? How very plebeian. Dred sifted through decades of friendship. Not even in high school did Dahlia go for the commonplace. Standout, one way or another. Dahlia's modus operandi. Was she ceding to time and age like everybody else? Making concessions? Rock solid Dahlia and her inexplicable, admirable, infuriating refusal to change actually relenting to the inevitable?

"What's going on?"

Dred jerked, Dahlia cringed at the rasping voice. Thunder Thighs stood stalwart and implacable above Dahlia. A wet towel almost circled Thunder's swimsuit. Her larger than life shadow drowned the prone and now worried Dahlia. The Hunk glanced up. "A slip and a fall." He capped the statement with a flash of dazzling pearly whites.

Thunder nearly swooned, but rallied, saying, "Again?"

Dahlia shot her a deadly glance. Suddenly, a gaggle of gabbling and babbling women surrounded Dahlia. The women's locker room had arrived en masse. Mr. Hunk, oblivious to the oglers, concentrated on prostrate Dahlia. "Why not confirm there's no injury by letting us take you to Emergency?" The locker room chorus repeated Emergency in a rising crescendo. Dahlia looked confused, rolling her head side to side. "I don't know."

Dred settled on her heels. Right. You don't know. The Hunk's physique and mystique muddled Dahlia's mind, confusing him with Jonathan the Missing, the husband who got away. Dred replayed the newsreel in her mind. Wounded and bewildered, Dahlia had immersed herself in the role of Wronged Wife even though she, herself, had plotted to fly off on a lark. But the lark got cold feet. Jonathan beat her out the door. Not only that, good old Jonathan did the unthinkable. He didn't grovel for forgiveness, but just kept right on going his merry way.

"Lucky she fell out here and not in the locker room," a chorister chimed.

"Yes." Dred shut her eyes to block the image: the squealing horde of women burdened by gravity, layered in loose skin scurrying to lockers, rushing to dress before Engine 39, maybe even The Hunk, arrived at the scene of the fall.

Dahlia propped herself onto an elbow, intent on Mr. Hunk. "I don't want to keep you...longer than necessary." She gazed into his blue eyes. "I so appreciate your attention."

"You're sure you don't want to go to Emergency?"

"Yes, yes, I'm sure." Dahlia breathed a long sigh. "Thank you, thank you oh so much." She put a hand on the runner to shove herself up. The Hunk reached over, deftly lifted her to her feet. Dahlia blessed him with a winsome smile, "I'm okay." The Hunk smiled a deep dimple and left.

Dred swallowed a sigh. The dimple was the killer, Jonathan lacked the cheek dent. "Well, Dahlia, now what?" Dred rested on one foot, arms akimbo.

"Why, home, Dred, home." Dahlia rotated the injured foot gingerly before putting weight on it. "It's fine, just fine." Pursing her lips in a pink pout, she gave the chorus a short shrug.

Thunder Thighs grimaced. "Nothing's wrong then."

Dahlia shook her head, fluffed her hair. Disappointed, the choristers headed for the locker room.

Dred approached the moment of truth. "Coming in I spotted Engine 39 parked outside. The guys were here to work out, weren't they?"

"Oh, really?" Dahlia stepped into her clogs.

"Did you trip?"

Dahlia adjusted her overblouse. "What do you think?"

PURPLE

Light touched the purple petal bending beneath the brush. For a moment the flower lived, then the light shifted. Mae dipped the paintbrush into a glass jar. Water softened the purple into lilac, then mauve swirls.

Her wrist hurt. She had allowed herself to flow into that water lily. The hours at the easel had slipped away, silent as night. She massaged each finger of her right hand. A simple gold band on her left ring finger snatched at sun.

She turned around to the picture window, its right edge graying like the day. She looked past the swimming pool, silent and inert, to the black wrought iron fence facing the park across the street. The green peace of trees and grass had soothed her when she and her husband, already an old man, first moved here. It soothed her still now that she was alone.

PAINTED TRAY

The curled lip of the tray fit within the curl of Claire's knobbed fingers. Joints too large, fingertips askew, each intent on going its own way. The hands of a woman grounded in the hard art of living the choices made in youth, preconceptions burned away in the hard light of perspective.

What Claire held in her hands unsettled her. She dipped the black oval toward the window, rinsed it in the meager light of sallow morning. Gold swirls trimmed the rim. Pale lines in thin white surfaced. Outlines of petals and leaves emerged at the far edges of a painted bouquet. Just a bit of flaking. Even with squinting she couldn't make out the numbers printed inside the exposed lines. Globs of coral red still clung to the rose centered in the metal tray. Probably toxic, Claire thought, remembering tiny vials of oil paint propped up in numbered holes punched into cardboard. Paint-by-number. About as original as sin.

She should have tossed it when they found it in the condo clutter. But Peter had played the guilt guitar, your mother kept it all these years. Claire caved, brought the tray home. Hid it. Peter, the self-appointed conscience of the family he had married into. Like any convert he was the most devout among them all in keeping a candle burning at the family altar. Had been, Claire corrected.

It was time. No one was left. She blocked light from her eyes, exhausted by the weight of remembered years. Milestones, that's what the caretakers—no, caregivers, in today's watered down parlance—called the accumulation of birthdays.

So here she was, at the window to a dead garden on a washed-out day dithering between April and May. The timing struck her. Wasn't this about when she had bought the paint-by-number set from Woolworth's? Mother's Day. She'd emptied the sock holding her savings for the Mother's Day after the autumn everyone moved out, leaving her and her mother alone. After school, painting, following instructions, following the colors pictured on the box. Recapping vials, replacing the tray in its cardboard cradle, hoping nothing would smear and the stench of turpentine wouldn't give her away. Shoving everything under the bed before her mother got home from work. A month after Mother's Day, her nighttime confession.

Claire let the tray fall to her side, moved toward the table to get away from the conversation. But she couldn't stop the flow. Not now, not then.

Tears had clutched her voice. Her mother sat on the beige sectional, sagging after only two years of being new. She sat as she always did, knees pulled up, feet together on the sofa, toes skimmed by her housecoat. Claire's tinny 12-year-old voice broke. I'm afraid you'll die. Leave.

Her mother sat. Dark eyes, deep silent wells. Then she spoke, soft, slow.

Miss my sisters? Claire stared. What was she talking about? They just got married one right after another. What was the connection between them leaving and her mother dying?

Her mother spoke again. Sadness tugged at her cheeks, shimmered in her eyes. You're lonely she said. Claire still didn't understand.

Claire banged the tray on the table. It shuddered, cracked the silence. An imperfect shield against what once was. Then the veneer of everyday years peeled away to an almost forgotten moment.

Back to a time when she was so small the two of them shared the big bed, the bed where her father once slept. She and her mother were playing Concentration, the cards face down on the blanket of bright squares her mother had crocheted with leftover yarn. Claire asked, asked just to ask, how many brothers and sisters do you have? Her mother looked at her with eyes burning with black anger. They sold me. My parents sold me. A rich family brought me to America. I cried and cried. I made myself forget. Forget how many brothers and sisters, she bent her left thumb. Forget their names, another finger went down. Their ages. My father's name. The village name. Her five folded fingers formed a fist. Everything. I was eight.

Bloodless sunlight pushed through the window. Claire smoothed a knobby hand, her mother's hand, across metal and paint wet with tears. Now she understood.

Foreshadowing

I return to whence I came. I leave no bloodline to trace, merely words written within the hourglass of my life, written to bear witness to what had been lived within the span of shared memory.

Some would say these worded memories of mine are exaggerated, inaccurate, willful. Untrue. Some would say more, these stories are betrayal. I think them truth, the truth that belongs to me. Imperfect as memory is, transitory as words are, they flow from the heart of me. The best I can give.

These remembrances given to me, I now pass on to you. Hold them as long as this memory bloodline withstands, until the sands smooth away my words, erase my name. A memory foreshadowed.

ABOUT THE AUTHOR

Rooted in the Midwest, transplanted to Friuli, Italy, and then to Marin County, California, Lum Franco is a longtime writer and intermittent traveler. She published *Segments,* a fictional memoir in 1996, authored short stories for *Bust Out Stories* and *Nearly Naked* and sundry other publications, large and small, as well scripted an award winning one-act play, *Salt.* She continues to write in Marin, sojourn in Friuli, and visit her roots in Chinatown.

To order additional copies
of *Backward Glance:*
www.amazon.com